## "David, I'm glad you're here," his mother said. "These two F.B.I. agents have a search warrant!"

His mother held up an envelope for him to see.

"The F.B.I.?" David echoed. For the first time, he noticed the cardboard boxes that were stacked up next to his bed. "What do they want with my computer?"

The man turned to David and said, "We're investigating a case of computer hacking. More than a hundred thousand dollars was stolen from a bank in the U.S. through the Internet, then transferred into a secret, numbered Swiss bank account yesterday."

"But what does that have to do with me?" David asked.

"We've been able to trace the hacker's origin, David," said the woman, Agent Kendall. "It led right to your computer."

# Wishbone™ Mysteries
## titles in Large-Print Editions:

# WISHBONE Mysteries

# CASE OF THE CYBER-HACKER

## by Anne Capeci

**WISHBONE**™ created by Rick Duffield

**Gareth Stevens Publishing**
A WORLD ALMANAC EDUCATION GROUP COMPANY

This book is a work of fiction. The characters, incidents, and dialogues are products of the author's imagination and are not to be construed as real. Any resemblance to actual events or persons, living or dead, is entirely coincidental.

For a free color catalog describing Gareth Stevens' list of high-quality books and multimedia programs, call 1-800-542-2595 (USA) or 1-800-461-9120 (Canada). Gareth Stevens Publishing's Fax: (414) 332-3567.

Library of Congress Cataloging-in-Publication Data

Capeci, Anne.
    Case of the cyber-hacker / by Anne Capeci ; [interior illustrations by
Lyle Miller].
        p. cm. — (The Wishbone mysteries; #19)
    Summary: When one of Wishbone's human friends is accused of computer
crime, it is up to the dog detective to find the real culprit.
    ISBN 0-8368-2702-3 (lib. bdg.)
    [1. Dogs—Fiction.  2. Internet (Computer network)—Fiction.  3. Mystery
and detective stories.]  I. Miller, Lyle, 1950-  ill.  II. Title.  III. Series.
    PZ7.C17363Cas   2000
    [Fic]—dc21                                                    00-029150

This edition first published in 2000 by
**Gareth Stevens Publishing**
A World Almanac Education Group Company
330 West Olive Street, Suite 100
Milwaukee, Wisconsin 53212 USA

© 2000 Big Feats Entertainment, L. P.  First published by Big Red Chair Books™, a Division of Lyrick Publishing™, 300 E. Bethany Drive, Allen, Texas 75002.

Edited by Kevin Ryan
Copy edited by Jonathon Brodman
Continuity editing by Grace Gantt
Cover concept and design by Lyle Miller
Interior illustrations by Lyle Miller
**Wishbone** photograph by Carol Kaelson

Printed in the United States of America

1 2 3 4 5 6 7 8 9 04 03 02 01 00

*For Isabella*

# FROM THE BIG RED CHAIR . . .

Oh . . . hi! Wishbone here. You caught me right in the middle of some of my favorite things—books. Let me welcome you to the WISHBONE Mysteries. In each story, I help my human friends solve a puzzling mystery. In *CASE OF THE CYBER-HACKER*, my next-door neighbor David Barnes is accused of computer-hacking by the F.B.I. Can my pals and I clear his name before a warrant is issued for his arrest?

The story takes place in the fall, during the same time period as the events that are featured in the second season of my WISHBONE television show. In this story, Joe is fifteen, and he and his friends are in the ninth grade. Like me, they are always ready for adventure . . . and a good mystery.

You're in for a real treat, so pull up a chair, grab a snack, and sink your teeth into *CASE OF THE CYBER-HACKER!*

# Chapter One

"**O**h, how I love the smells of a sunny afternoon in the park!" Wishbone sniffed the fresh air as he trotted along on the green grass of Jackson Park. "Flowers, earth, leaves . . . It's all enough to make a dog long for adventure!"

The white-with-black-and-brown-spots Jack Russell terrier felt the first hint of an autumn chill on his fur. It energized him so much that he kicked up his paws and raced across the grass. He barked a greeting to a woman jogging on one of the paths that wound through the park. But the person Wishbone most wanted to see and play with was nowhere in sight.

"Joe? Where are you, buddy!" Wishbone's very best friend, Joe Talbot, liked the park as much as Wishbone did. They had spent long days there during the summer playing ball and running free—often with their friends David Barnes and Samantha Kepler. But now that Joe had started high school, he had many more responsibilities. He wasn't free to play anymore until late in the afternoon.

Wishbone turned to look toward the sun. Its low angle told him the day was moving on.

"It won't be long now! And in the meantime . . ."— Wishbone raced to his favorite old oak tree in a woodsy area and pawed at the soft earth among its roots— ". . . this dog's gotta dig!"

The dirt smelled strongly with the scents of Wishbone's canine pals from all over Oakdale. But as he dug up the soft earth, his sensitive nose picked up an interesting new smell.

"A new dog in town? Great!" He trotted out to the edge of the woods, his tail wagging. "Helllooo! Where are you?"

Wishbone didn't see any canines among the many trees and bushes. He barked to let the other dog know he was there. But the only answer he heard was the sound of the breeze rustling the tree branches above. Why didn't the dog come out?

"There's a mystery dog nearby." Wishbone trotted back into the woods, keeping his eyes and ears alert. "And no one likes a good mystery as much as I do. . . ."

David Barnes walked down the first-floor hallway of Wilson High School on Wednesday afternoon. Classes were over for the day. Boys and girls flooded toward the exit doors. They pulled on their jackets and slung their backpacks over their shoulders as they made their way out. The sunny day was tempting. But David was headed for completely different territory: cyberspace.

He pushed open the door to the computer lab, then smiled. Everything in there was so familiar: the terminals lining the walls, the sounds of fingers tapping on computer keyboards, the letters and graphics appearing on the glowing screens. There, David was in the world he loved and knew so well.

"Hi, everyone," he said to the four students who sat close together at the front of the room.

Joanna Finlay, the president of the Wilson Computer Club, looked up and smiled. She was seventeen, and a senior. She had thoughtful-looking brown eyes and chin-length brown hair that she kept tucked behind her ears. David had met her a few weeks earlier, after starting his first year at Wilson High.

"Hi, David," Joanna said. "Glad you could make it. You're the last one here, so I guess now we can get started."

David quickly looked at the faces of the other members of the club. Shawn O'Brian had wiry red hair and a good sense of humor. He and Elena Rivera, a girl with a wide smile and straight dark hair, were both juniors, and sixteen years old. David didn't know them very well yet.

But the final member of the group, a boy with swept-back blond hair who wore round-framed eyeglasses, was someone David had known since middle school. It was Gilbert Stuart Pickering. He was a freshman, like David. Both were fourteen. The two boys had something else in common, too—they were fascinated by everything that was high-tech.

"Did you take a crack at the challenge?" Gilbert asked, as David took a seat next to him.

Gilbert's eyes shone with excitement, and David understood why. After all, it wasn't every day that a mysterious Internet surfer tested their cyber-skills. Just one week earlier, someone using the code name "Top-Dog" had logged on to the Computer Club's chat room. TopDog had asked a lot of questions about the club and the software programs that its members used. David had been very interested when TopDog issued a challenge: Could any of the club's members make a message appear on someone else's computer screen?

"I've got my program right here," David said. He unzipped the front pocket of his backpack and pulled out a computer disk.

The challenge was much harder than just sending a message to another computer by e-mail. The message would have to go right to the other computer without passing through an electronic "mailbox" or a chat room first. These two forms of communication were the most common ways of sending messages. David was pleased with what he had come up with.

"I created a message, too," Joanna said. She looked at her watch. "TopDog will be logging on in five minutes to get our results. How did all of you do?"

"I didn't get anywhere," said Shawn, shaking his head.

"Me, either," said Elena. "What software can do that?"

"DynameX," Gilbert said. "Wait till you see the message I programmed by using it."

David had used DynameX to program his message, as well. The cutting-edge computer-programming language was still being tested by its creators. But David had managed to get a preview, or "beta," copy through the Internet. David didn't fully understand it yet, but he liked what he had learned about it so far. With DynameX, it was possible to make an image or a message or a whole screen appear on another computer.

"A message can only be as clever as its creator." Joanna grinned as she took a computer disk from her own backpack. She tapped it, looking from Gilbert to David with eyes that were full of anticipation. "You're not going to believe my message."

"Let's see if TopDog has logged on yet," Gilbert said.

David watched while Joanna logged on to the Internet. She typed in the address of the Computer Club's Web site. Within seconds, the words "WILSON HIGH CYBER-CAVE" spelled themselves out in 3-D geometric neon letters. Joanna clicked on the "Talk" icon. The chat room appeared on the screen right away. David looked at the left side of the screen, where the names of all the people who were logged on to the chat room were listed.

"TopDog is already here," he said.

Instantly, a message from TopDog appeared on the screen: WHERE'VE U BEEN? ANYONE GOT THE MUSCLE 2 MEET MY CHALLENGE?

A smile broke out on Joanna's lips as she typed her response: PIECE OF CAKE. THREE WINNERS: BIGBROTHER, TRAILBLAZ-R, AND WIZKID.

Everyone used code names on the Internet. David had a younger sister, Emily, so he had chosen "Big-Brother" as his code name. Joanna was "Trailblaz-R," and Gilbert was "WizKid."

"You're first, David!" Joanna said.

David went to another terminal. He sat down, slid his disk into the drive, and tapped a few commands. "Mine's an Easter egg," he told the others.

An "Easter egg" referred to a hidden message that

had been programmed to appear on someone else's computer when the person using the computer did something out of the ordinary.

"Click on the 'Okay' box three times," David told Joanna.

When she did, the word "SURPRISE!" scrolled across the screen in bright colors, along with the sound effects of fireworks and moving images of all the kids in the Computer Club—Shawn, Elena, Gilbert, Joanna, and David. The message also appeared at the same time on the Wilson Computer Club's chat room. As the photographic images slowly faded, a second message flashed on the bottom of the screen in neon letters surrounded by spiraling, multicolored helixes: THIS MESSAGE HAS BEEN BROUGHT TO YOU BY BIGBROTHER. This special message is used to identify the sender and is known as a signature.

"Cool," Gilbert said.

It seemed that TopDog thought so, too. His message appeared on the screen moments later: TOUGH ACT 2 FOLLOW, BB. CAN ANYONE TOP IT?

Joanna and Gilbert both tried. Joanna had created a "Happy Birthday" message, complete with noise-makers, a birthday cake, and balloons that floated across the screen. Gilbert's message showed two knights in armor having a jousting contest. David thought they were both great.

After they were all through sending their messages, TopDog typed out: MY VOTE GOES 2 BB. HOW DO U GUYS VOTE?

Joanna, Gilbert, Shawn, and Elena looked at one another. "I don't think we even need to vote," Joanna said. "Does everyone agree that David is the winner?"

There were nods all around. "You really went all out, David," Gilbert said. "That signature was a nice touch."

"The animation must have taken you forever to put together," Shawn added.

"I liked doing it," David said, shrugging. "I figured I might as well take the challenge to the limit—you know, just to see what I could do."

David was very modest about his computer abilities, but it felt good to see Joanna type a message declaring him the winner of the challenge. Joanna added David's winning program to the club's Web site.

Next, Joanna logged back on to the chat room to say good-bye to TopDog: THANKS FOR THE CHALLENGE, TD. DON'T B A STRANGER, OKAY?

TopDog's answer appeared instantly: WANT 2 TRY SOMETHING TOUGHER? CREATE A GAME U CAN PLAY ON THE COMPUTER OF SOMEONE U KNOW, BY USING REMOTE CONTROL.

"Sounds like fun," David said. "It would double the challenge because we would have to send the game to another computer *and* get control of the other computer so we can play the game. Are you up for it?"

"Definitely." Joanna's eyes shone with excitement as she looked at the others. "We could each pick someone else in the club. Is everyone up for this next challenge?"

David, Elena, Gilbert, and Shawn all nodded. Joanna turned back to the keyboard and typed: YOU'RE ON!

TopDog's final message showed up on the screen:

C U NEXT WEEK. SAME TIME, SAME PLACE. BLASTING OFF 4 ZONDOR!

A moment later, TopDog's name disappeared as he logged off.

"'Blasting off for Zondor'?" Elena said, arching an eyebrow. "What does that mean?"

David shook his head. "It's just TopDog's way of saying good-bye, I guess. He used it last week, too."

The meeting was breaking up, so David put his computer disk in his backpack. Then he got up and headed for the door. Gilbert caught up with him as he stepped into the hallway.

"David, remember my Uncle Max?" Gilbert asked.

"Sure," David answered. He had met Gilbert's uncle when he was trying to learn the truth about a mysterious aircraft that had crash-landed on the outskirts of Oakdale. A lot of locals had suspected it might be an alien spaceship, a UFO. But David was fairly sure it had been an experimental aircraft being developed by Littleton Aerospace, a company where Max Pickering worked as an aeronautical engineer.

"Uncle Max told me Littleton's computer department is holding a conference next summer," Gilbert said. "They'll need an intern to help out, but my family's going to be camping at the Grand Canyon then. Uncle Max asked if you'd be interested."

"That sounds great!" David said, thrilled by the idea. Littleton Aerospace was one of the best aerospace technology companies in the country. "Tell your uncle I'm definitely interested."

David smiled as he walked toward the exit. He'd won TopDog's challenge and gotten a lead on a terrific job as a computer intern, all in one day. *Not bad,* he thought. *Not bad at all.*

The late-afternoon sunshine felt good on David's face as he headed into Jackson Park after leaving the Wilson High School computer lab. His two best friends, Samantha Kepler and Joe Talbot, had told him earlier they would be playing ball in the park after school let out for the day. Sam was outgoing, creative, and always ready to reach out and lend others a helping hand. Joe was David's next-door neighbor. Sports was Joe's main thing, especially basketball. David waved when he caught sight of them on one of the wide, grassy lawns.

"Sam! Joe!" he called.

Sam had just finished batting the baseball. As she turned to look at David, her blond hair swung from side to side. Beneath the brim of her baseball cap, her blue eyes flashed as she smiled. "Your meeting is over already?" she asked.

Across the field, Joe had caught the ball. He was taller than David, with brown hair and eyes, and an athletic build. Joe's dog, Wishbone, was sniffing at some bushes nearby. Just as Joe's hands had closed around the ball, the terrier raced over. He grabbed the baseball in his muzzle and gave it a playful tug.

"Down, boy," Joe said. He pulled the ball free and threw it in David's direction. "Think fast!"

David dropped his backpack and got ready to catch the ball. "Our meeting broke up after we decided who'd won that challenge I told you about," he said.

David had already told Sam and Joe about meeting TopDog on-line. Now, as the three friends sat on the grass, he filled them in on the latest news.

"You won? Way to go!" Joe said.

"So this guy just logged on to your Web site and offered you a challenge?" Sam asked.

"Right," David answered. "Lots of people surf the Internet and choose different Web sites. And everyone uses code names."

"I guess that's part of the fun of it, huh?" Joe said. But Sam didn't look convinced.

"I don't think I would want to talk to someone that I met through a chat room and didn't really know," she said, frowning. "Doesn't that bother you, David?"

David didn't have to think twice about his answer. "Nope," he said. "I like keeping some parts of my life private."

"I can understand that," said Joe.

David felt a pull on the baseball, which he still held in one hand. Wishbone nudged it with his muzzle, looking at David with what seemed like begging eyes. "Okay, okay," David said. He stood up and threw the ball in a long, high arc. His eyes followed Wishbone as the terrier chased it into the bushes. The dog found the ball, then dropped it to sniff among the bushes again.

"Come on, Wishbone!" Joe called.

David turned back to look at his friends. He saw Sam gazing down at the grass thoughtfully. "I guess because the Internet lets the user be secretive, it is kind of exciting," she said slowly. "And mysterious."

"Not as mysterious as the book I'm reading now," David said.

"You started reading *The Thirty-Nine Steps*?" Joe asked.

David wasn't surprised to see a spark of interest in his friend's eyes. After all, Joe was the one who had lent David the mystery story.

"*The Thirty-Nine Steps*?" Sam echoed. "I've never heard of it." She clapped her hands as Wishbone came running back with the ball. Taking it from him, she threw it out again.

"It's a thriller," David told her. "A British author named John Buchan wrote it. It's about this guy, Richard Hannay."

"What's so mysterious about him?" Sam wanted to know.

"The book starts out in London, England, just before the beginning of World War One," David explained. "Hannay is minding his own business when a stranger, Franklin Scudder, comes up to him. Scudder tells Hannay that members of an underground political group are after him."

"The Black Stone is the name of the group," Joe

18

added. "Scudder thinks they're trying to kill him."

"Why?" Sam asked.

"Scudder says the Black Stone is planning to murder an important political figure," David answered. "That would probably set off a world war. Even though Scudder is a total stranger, Hannay believes him. He lets Scudder hide in his apartment and promises to do what he can to help."

"And?" Sam prompted. David could see that the story had caught her interest. She didn't even notice that Wishbone had returned with the baseball and had dropped it on the grass in front of them.

"A few days later, Hannay finds Franklin Scudder stabbed to death in Hannay's apartment," David went on. "Hannay is sure the Black Stone did it, and he'll be the prime suspect, so he takes off."

"Hannay is on the run from the police and the Black Stone," Joe added.

"Wow!" Sam said. "That *is* a major mystery."

David nodded. "I haven't read any further than that, so I don't know what happens next," he said.

"And I'm not about to spoil the suspense," Joe said, grinning.

Sam finally noticed Wishbone and the ball. She reached out to pick up the baseball. Then she turned to David with a smile. "At least you don't have to worry about the stranger, TopDog, getting you involved in something like that," she said.

David glanced at the grassy lawns and wooded trails of Jackson Park. "That's for sure," he agreed. "The

19

chances of a major conspiracy happening around here are pretty slim."

"Excuse me, but I think there is a major conspiracy right here," Wishbone said. "A conspiracy to ignore the dog!"

Wishbone was also familiar with the story of *The Thirty-Nine Steps*. Thinking of Richard Hannay's hair-raising adventures made Wishbone think of the puzzle in his own life.

"Anyone seen a strange dog around here?" Wishbone gazed up at his friends, then sighed. "I guess not. Okay, then let's keep playing!" He took hold of the ball with his teeth and gave a tug. "Please?"

"Okay, Wishbone," Sam said. She pulled the baseball free of his muzzle and threw it toward the trees.

"Yes!" Wishbone raced forward, keeping his eyes on the spinning white ball. When it disappeared into the woods, Wishbone ran after it. "No problem. We canines are expert at tracking in the wilderness. I wouldn't be surprised if Richard Hannay received his basic training from one of my ancestors."

As Wishbone ran, he caught another whiff of the canine scent he'd been picking up all afternoon.

"There it is again. And this time it's even stronger!" He stopped running and sniffed at the ivy beneath his paws. "The mystery dog must be—"

Wishbone turned suddenly toward a clump of bushes to his left. He'd heard something—a rustling noise. Panting, he took a step closer.

"Aha!" Wishbone grinned when he saw the gray coat and slender muzzle of a greyhound that stepped from the bushes. "So there you are! I've been looking all over for you!"

With his tail wagging, Wishbone trotted toward the greyhound. He didn't see any collar or tags, but the greyhound looked as if he had a home. He smelled okay and his coat wasn't too dirty. Judging by the dog's scent and the white hairs that flecked his muzzle and paws, he was an older dog. As the terrier looked more closely, he saw that the old dog had bloodshot eyes.

"Hey, you're shaking! Are you sick?" Wishbone moved closer and touched the greyhound's nose with his own. It was feverishly hot and dry. "You shouldn't be out here all by yourself. You need help!"

Wishbone spotted the look of caution in the greyhound's eyes.

"I know you're scared. But you don't have to worry about me. The name's Wishbone, and I'm at your service. My friends are, too."

The terrier let out a series of ringing barks, sounding the alarm.

"Joe! Sam! David! I need backup here!"

Moments later the three kids came running toward him. Joe was in the lead. "Wishbone? What's the matter, boy?" he called. His face was tight with worry as he pushed aside some branches and made his way toward Wishbone.

"Check it out. There's another dog," David said, as he and Sam came up behind Joe. David paused a few feet away from Wishbone and the greyhound. "No collar or tags. Do you think it's a stray?"

"He needs help!" Wishbone barked, jumping around his friends' feet.

Slowly, Sam came forward, holding out her hand to the greyhound. "It's all right. I'm not going to hurt you, boy. Don't be scared. . . ."

Wishbone saw every muscle in the greyhound's body tighten. He tried to back away. But as soon as he took a step, he stumbled and fell.

"He's hurt!" Sam jumped forward to help the dog. "He's shaking. And his nose feels really warm. Those are signs of sickness in dogs."

Joe nodded. "They sure are. I don't think he's a stray. He doesn't look like he has been on his own. But . . ." He turned to look around, his hands on his hips. "Where could his owner be?"

Wishbone gave another urgent bark. "Help the dog first, guys! We'll find his family later!"

"He needs help," David said. He crouched down, trying to steady the greyhound as the dog attempted to stand again.

Joe stared down at the greyhound for a long moment. Then he nodded his head, as if he'd just decided something. "I'm going to take him home," he said. "You guys stay here. I'll find a pay phone and call my mom."

"Excellent idea, Joe!" Wishbone said. As Joe jogged out of the woods, the terrier licked his new friend's sleek fur. "Didn't I tell you? Help is on the way!"

Finally! David thought, as he closed his algebra book after dinner that night.

It had been tough to focus on his homework. He kept thinking about the old greyhound that he, Sam, Joe, and Wishbone had found in the woods. Ellen Talbot, Joe's mom, had driven to the park in her Ford Explorer to take the dog home. David was glad to know the dog was in good hands.

"Now for some cyber-thrills and chills . . ."

David set aside his math book and turned on the computer in his bedroom. This was the first chance he'd had to zero in on TopDog's latest challenge.

*Create a game,* he thought, as the machine beeped and hummed to life. *One that can be played on someone else's computer . . .*

Playing a game on someone else's computer was hard, but not impossible, especially now that David had mastered the basics of DynameX. The more he used it, the more he learned.

The tricky part would be getting remote-control access to the other computer so he could play the game.

"Here goes . . ."

David decided to use Gilbert's computer as his target

for the challenge. Before long, he created a game and succeeded in sending it to Gilbert's computer. But playing the game was much harder. David experimented with DynameX, playing with different commands and keying them in different orders. But . . .

"No go," he muttered. He still hadn't learned the trick of playing the game by using remote control.

David's fingers flew over the keyboard as he tried yet again. Surely there was something he had overlooked. He typed in a new command, ran the program, and . . .

"Huh?" David blinked as a list of computer files appeared on his screen. None of the file names was familiar. He squinted, reading them aloud. "'Games.gil,' 'WizKid'" . . .

David couldn't believe his eyes.

"Hey!" He did a double take when he recognized the code name Gilbert used on the Internet. "These must be Gilbert's files!"

He had gained access to Gilbert's computer—not just to the controls, but to all of Gilbert's files, as well!

"It can't be!" David said, shaking his head firmly. There had to be some kind of blocking feature that would prevent him from opening the files.

David highlighted the file called "Games.gil" and pressed the key to open it. He waited for the message that would tell him access was denied. But, instead . . .

"Whoa!" David sat bolt upright as a list of computer games came up on his screen.

He couldn't believe what had just happened.

What a major loophole! This small opening through DynameX could allow him to get into people's computers . . . illegally. He had gained total access to Gilbert's computer!

A shiver ran down David's spine. Quickly, he exited the file and stopped the program he had created with DynameX. Then he stared at his screen while he thought.

Using DynameX, a person could break into any computer. A keyboarder could change records, destroy files, turn off alarm systems—anything he or she wanted to do!

"I have to warn the other kids in the Computer Club," David said.

He logged on to the Internet and posted a message about the loophole on the Wilson High Cyber-Cave Web site: DANGEROUS LOOPHOLE IN DYNAMEX. GIVES TOTAL ACCESS TO TARGET COMPUTER. . . . PROCEED WITH CAUTION.

# Chapter Two

"I guess the double dose of kibble Ellen gave you this morning did the trick." It was early Thursday morning. Wishbone turned in the backseat of Ellen's parked Ford Explorer to look at the greyhound.

The old dog was still stiff and unsteady on his feet. But Wishbone was glad to see that the greyhound was no longer shaking and feverish.

Still, even though he was better, the greyhound didn't seem completely comfortable. He followed Wishbone's every move with watchful eyes.

"Don't you know by now that Joe and Ellen and I want to help?" Wishbone said. "We're doing our best to find your family."

Ellen and Joe were walking along Oak Street, taping "Lost Dog" signs on trees, telephone poles, and in store windows. Wishbone wagged his tail when he saw them return to the Explorer a few minutes later. "We've put up posters just about everywhere, including Beck's

Grocery, Jack's Service Station, and every store on Oak Street," Joe said, as he got into the front seat. "Anyone who comes to town will see one."

Ellen slid in behind the steering wheel and started the car. "Too bad the greyhound's owner didn't put up any signs," she said. "That would have made our job easier. It's a good thing we had enough paper to make up all those signs last night." She glanced at her watch before pulling into traffic. "Well, we'd better get you to school, Joe."

Ellen turned off Oak Street, passing the First Commercial Bank of Oakdale and Oakdale Attic Antiques as they headed out of the shopping district. Wishbone kept his head close to the open window, taking in the whole scene. He thumped his tail against the seat as he caught whiffs of the crisp autumn air, grass, and trees.

All of a sudden, the greyhound jumped up to stand next to Wishbone. A high-pitched whine escaped from the back of his throat. It was almost as if . . .

"You know this place, don't you!" Wishbone turned to his new friend in surprise. "Joe! Ellen!"

Joe glanced over the back of his seat. "Something's wrong, Mom," he said, frowning at the greyhound. "Maybe you should stop."

Wishbone saw Ellen's concerned eyes reflected in the rearview mirror. She turned into the parking lot of the Royal Theater and pulled the Explorer to a stop. As soon as she opened her door, the greyhound scrambled over the seat back and across Ellen's lap. Then he leaped outside.

"He's still not completely well," Ellen said, as she unstrapped her seat belt and got out. "I'm afraid he'll get hurt."

"I'll get him!" Joe called.

Wishbone was already jumping to the front seat and out the door. "Ditto for the dog. I'm on his trail, Ellen!" He heard Joe's sneakers crunch on the gravel behind him.

The greyhound was moving pretty fast. He managed to make his way across the parking lot ahead of Wishbone. He ran across the street, stopping briefly to sniff at the roots of an oak tree. The old dog continued for two blocks and then scrambled through a patch of rhododendron bushes. The greyhound seemed to know exactly where he was going.

"This way, Joe!"

Wishbone ran through the rhododendron bushes. When he came out into sunlight a moment later, he found himself at the edge of a driveway that led to a modern building that looked as if it had once been an old barn. Wishbone spotted a weathervane and what had once been a hayloft. Huge picture windows had been cut into the weathered boards on the sides of the barn. A neon sign glowed behind one plate-glass panel.

"Is this where you're from?" Wishbone called out to the greyhound.

Up ahead, the old dog ran toward the building. Wishbone was surprised when two more greyhounds came racing from around a newer-looking garage that stood behind the building. These greyhounds were much younger. All three dogs sniffed and barked at one another like long-lost friends.

"That clinches it!" Wishbone turned as Joe and Ellen caught up to him. "Take a look, guys. I'd say he's found his family!"

"Check it out, Mom. This must be his home," Joe said, nodding at the three dogs.

Wishbone gave a sigh. "Didn't I just say that?"

"ToonTime Graphix," Ellen said, pausing to read the neon sign in the window. "Let's go in and see if we can find the owner."

Wishbone followed her and Joe to the sliding-glass door that had replaced the original barn doors. As they stepped inside, the three greyhounds followed.

Wishbone stopped next to the door to look around. Different desks and machines were placed all over in the huge, open space. Wishbone's alert eyes picked out potted plants, a couch that looked perfect for snoozing, and even a kitchen area. A metal staircase led up along one wall to a loft area above.

Everything looked pleasant enough. Yet there was something about the place he didn't like. As he looked around, a sudden ice-cold shiver made his fur stand on end.

Wishbone caught sight of two men in the office. They were working at a machine that contained a large screen and a control panel covered with knobs and buttons. The young man seated in front of the machine was in his early twenties, with thick, wavy light-brown hair. The other man was older, with straight blond hair. Both were staring at the screen with the kind of deep concentration Wishbone used when searching for long-buried bones. Neither man seemed to have noticed that anyone else was there.

"Excuse me, sir," Joe spoke up, stepping toward the men. "I'm Joe Talbot. Is this your dog? My friends and I found him in Jackson Park yesterday."

"I'm Joe's mom, Ellen Talbot," Ellen said.

The two men looked up in surprise. Upon seeing the greyhound, the older man blinked. Then he smiled and walked over to shake hands with Joe and Ellen. "I'm Hal Bolton. I own ToonTime Graphix," he said. He nodded back toward the younger man and said, "That's Corey Anderson, my assistant."

The young man gave a quick wave before turning his attention back to the screen.

"Lightning is mine, all right," Hal Bolton went on. "At least, he's been mine since my sister moved to Zenith and couldn't take her dogs with her." He shook his head. "He wandered off after I gave him a bath the other day. Thanks for bringing him back, Joe. I was starting to think he was gone for good."

As Hal Bolton walked toward Lightning, the old dog gave a nervous jump. He stumbled as the man patted him on the head.

"I guess he's still kind of shaky," Joe said to Bolton. "He was sick when we found him."

Wishbone's canine instincts told him that Lightning's shaking wasn't caused by any sickness. Looking at the two other greyhounds, he saw that they, too, were keeping a careful distance from Bolton. Wishbone sat back on his haunches and stared at the man.

"You guys are afraid of him," Wishbone said. The icy feeling that had gotten under his fur grew stronger. "This man should be your best buddy. But you're acting as if he's about to give you a shot. There must be a reason why—and I'm going to find out what it is!"

While Bolton talked with Joe and Ellen, Wishbone sniffed around the open work area, catching a whiff of . . .

"Food dishes!" Wishbone's mouth started to water when he spotted the two dog dishes and water bowls in the kitchen area. He went over and lapped up some water, then sat back and cocked his head to the side. "But . . . shouldn't there be *three* dishes?"

Wishbone decided to investigate and climbed the stairway to the loft. Part of the loft was walled off to form an office. There was a desk with a computer on it overlooking the work space below. As Wishbone stepped inside the office, his nails clicked on the wood floor.

"Let's see. . . . Another machine, some old newspapers . . . Those would age perfectly if they were buried for a few days."

Wishbone peeked over the top of the trash bin that stood next to the desk. He looked inside.

"A plastic food dish! It must belong to Lightning. It has his smell. But why would Bolton— Hey!"

Wishbone yelped as someone yanked on his collar, lifting him up. The next thing he knew, he was staring

into Hal Bolton's steely gray eyes. The man didn't say a word. But the look in his eyes made Wishbone shiver. The terrier tried to squirm free, but Bolton kept a firm hold on him.

"Wishbone? Where are you, boy?" Joe's voice came from downstairs.

Bolton quickly shoved the trash bin out of sight under his desk. Then he carried Wishbone back down-stairs, where Ellen and Joe were waiting.

"I thought I heard something up in my office," Bolton said. He smiled broadly and handed Wishbone over to Joe. "Thought I'd better bring him back down before he breaks something."

Wishbone was happy to find himself in the safety of Joe's arms. "This man is bad news!" he said, barking sharply. "He threw away Lightning's dish. Just take a look up——"

"I don't know what's gotten into Wishbone,"

Ellen said. "He seems upset. I'm sorry he wandered into your office, Mr. Bolton."

"No harm done," Bolton said. "Thanks again for returning Lightning."

"Don't let that smile fool you!" Wishbone kept barking.

Joe and Ellen simply said good-bye to Hal Bolton. Joe carried Wishbone tightly as he and his mom headed back the way they had come.

"You haven't seen the last of me! There is something suspicious here," Wishbone said over Joe's shoulder at Bolton. "I'll be back. You can count on it!"

"Are you trying to tell me there's actually a computer program that lets you get access into someone else's computer?" Joe asked David, as they walked home from school that afternoon. "Is that legal?"

"Probably not," David answered. "I'm pretty sure it's something the creators of DynameX didn't plan on."

Joe's eyes widened in disbelief. "You mean, it's a mistake? How is that possible?" he asked.

"It happens," David said, shrugging. "Computer programs are really complicated. The designers aren't always aware of everything the programs can do. DynameX is brand-new. It'll take time to get all the bugs worked out. That's why companies use beta testing before they ship a new program to stores."

"That seems kind of dangerous," Joe said.

"That's what I've been thinking," David replied. "I'm going to e-mail the company when I get home."

"Can I watch you?" Joe asked.

"Sure," David told him.

As the two boys reached David's house, Wishbone came tearing across the street from Joe's yard.

"Hey, boy," Joe said, scratching Wishbone behind his ears.

David glanced at the green minivan that was parked in his driveway. It didn't look familiar, but he didn't think anything special of it. Walking past, David led the way through his garage workshop, where he did most of his mechanical tinkering.

When David opened the door to the kitchen, Wishbone ran inside ahead of him and Joe. David wasn't surprised when the terrier looked up at the platter of cookies sitting at the edge of the counter. Wishbone had great radar when it came to detecting food.

"David, is that you?" Mrs. Barnes called from upstairs.

"Yes, Mom. And Joe's here, too," David called back.

"You'd better come up here." There was a strained tone in his mother's voice.

David and Joe hurried up the carpeted stairs. When they reached the landing, David saw a man and a woman in his room with his mother. The man was about his mother's age, with slicked-back dark hair and dark eyes. The woman had short blond hair and freckles. They were both dressed in dark business suits.

David did a double take when he saw that the man was unplugging his printer cable. The boy stepped forward and asked, "What are you doing?"

"David, I'm glad you're here," his mother said. "These are F.B.I. agents Kendall and Guardi. They have a search warrant!" His mother held up an envelope for him to see.

"The F.B.I.?" David echoed. For the first time, he noticed the cardboard boxes that were stacked up next to his bed. "What do they want with my computer?"

The man turned to David and said, "We're investigating a case of computer hacking. More than a hundred thousand dollars was stolen from a bank in the U.S. through the Internet, then transferred into a secret, numbered Swiss bank account yesterday."

"But what does that have to do with me?" David asked.

"We've been able to trace the hacker's origin, David," said the woman, Agent Kendall. "It led right to your computer."

# Chapter Three

"**M**y pal David would never do anything illegal!" Wishbone trotted into David's room and gave an angry bark. "Someone's made a big mistake here!"

Agent Guardi stepped right past Wishbone and reached for one of the cardboard boxes. "We're going to have to confiscate your computer, David," he said.

"Take my computer? But I didn't steal any money!" David insisted.

"We've been checking up on you," said Agent Kendall. "This isn't the first contact you've had with the F.B.I."

"Agent Kendall, that was all a mistake. David was innocent," said Mrs. Barnes.

Wishbone knew that David had transferred millions of dollars using his computer when he was in sixth grade. "Right. It was an accident! Tell them, David!"

Agents Guardi and Kendall didn't even look at

Wishbone. They just continued packing up David's computer system.

"No one ever listens to the dog."

"How can you think I stole this money you're talking about?"

Wishbone recognized the looks on the faces of the F.B.I. agents. It was the same way Wanda looked at Wishbone when she caught him digging among her petunias. "The person who transferred the money put his signature on the programming he used," said Agent Guardi, as he scooped up the CDs and discs on David's desk. "The signature was yours."

David blinked in surprise. "But you use a signature when you want other people to know you're responsible," he said. David knew this because he had created his own signature for the surprise message he'd shown TopDog and the Computer Club the day before.

"That's right," said Agent Guardi.

"So why would I use a signature if I didn't want to get caught?" David went on. "That would be like signing my name to the crime!"

Agent Kendall shook her head as she taped up the box containing David's monitor. "How else would your friends know that you pulled off the heist?" she said. "You may have thought it was all a joke, but people go to jail for committing computer fraud."

"Jail!" Wishbone barked. "But David is innocent. I already told you that!"

He caught the sober looks that passed between David, Joe, and David's mother. "Anyone who knows my signature could have used it," David protested. "Someone else must have set me up."

Ruth Barnes slipped an arm around David's shoulders. "I'm sure my son is telling the truth," she told the F.B.I. agents. "What about that person you met on-line, David? Someone with a name like TopGun . . . or . . . TopDog. Isn't that his name?"

Both F.B.I. agents looked at David, waiting for his answer. "Can you tell us more?" asked Agent Kendall.

"It's just someone I talked to on-line," David said, crossing his arms over his chest.

Wishbone saw a closed expression come over David's face. It was a look Wishbone had seen before, when David was keeping something to himself.

Agent Kendall stared at David for a long moment. "If there's something you want to tell us, this would be a good time," she said. When David said nothing, she looked at him for a few seconds and added, "Are you protecting someone, David?"

Wishbone looked up at David. "What's so secret about this TopDog person, David?" He sighed when David simply stood there in silence.

"Breaking into private files is a serious federal crime, David," Agent Guardi said. "We consider this kind of cyber-attack a major threat. An attack on American cyberspace is an attack on the United States. It's terrorism."

"Whoa!" Wishbone trotted over to sniff the cardboard box that contained David's computer.

David's mother turned to face the two agents.

"My son's told you he didn't steal that money. Where else are you looking?"

Agent Guardi took another long look at David. "We'll be back in two days. There's a good chance we'll have a warrant for your arrest by then. I suggest you contact your lawyer."

"We're building a case against you," Agent Kendall added. "And right now, it looks pretty strong."

The two agents began to carry the boxes outside to their van. David, his mom, Joe, and Wishbone walked outside and watched the action.

Twenty minutes later, the F.B.I. agents had loaded half a dozen cardboard boxes into their minivan. Agent Guardi said to David, as he got in behind the wheel, "If you think of anything you'd like to tell us, you can reach us at the Oakdale Inn."

Wishbone watched the green minivan drive out of sight. Then he glanced up at David, who was staring after the van with serious eyes.

"I've got two days to prove I'm innocent," David said.

"What are you going to do?" Joe asked. "You don't even have your computer."

"Or my software . . . or any of my computer manuals. They even took my stereo and Dad's electronic address book!" David said.

"The search warrant authorized them to take any electronic device that stores information," said David's mother. She gave his shoulder a squeeze, then turned back to the house. "Don't worry, David. I'm calling

your father now. Just try to be patient until we can talk to a lawyer about what to do."

Wishbone saw the determined look on David's face. "Call it a canine instinct. Something tells me that being patient isn't a part of your plan, David. . . ."

There's nothing like the smell of a pepperoni pizza with extra cheese." Wishbone eagerly sniffed the air as he, Joe, and David walked into Pepper Pete's Pizza Parlor at five o'clock. After the F.B.I. had left the Barneses' house, Joe had suggested that he and David speak to Sam. "Coming here to talk to Sam was a great idea. Pizza ought to make you feel better, David. It always does the trick for me."

Wishbone glanced around as he, David, and Joe sat in one of the booths by the windows. His mouth began to water when he saw the pepperoni pizza Sam was setting down on a table across the room. Sam's father owned Pepper Pete's, and she often helped out there after school. It was an arrangement Wishbone found most appealing—and appetizing—especially since Sam almost always found extra scraps for the dog.

"Hi, guys!" Sam smiled as she came over to their booth. She tucked her order pad in her apron pocket and slid into the booth next to David. "What's up?"

David, Joe, and Wishbone told her the story of what had just happened at David's house. Sam's face grew more and more serious as she listened.

"You mean, the F.B.I. thinks you broke into that bank's computer files and transferred money illegally?" she asked.

David nodded. "I've got to come up with a plan to clear my name," he said. His dark eyes still held the determined gleam Wishbone had seen back at his house. "That's why Joe and I came over here. Maybe the three of us can come up with a plan."

"And me, too!" Wishbone said. "Don't forget about the dog, folks!"

"Let's start from the beginning," Sam said. "You think someone used your signature to set you up."

"That's right. I think I know who it is, too," David said. "The first time I ever even used a signature was when I made up that surprise message for TopDog's challenge. The only people who saw the signature were the other kids in the Computer Club and—"

43

"TopDog," Joe finished.

David nodded. "I can't believe any of the kids in the club would set me up," he went on.

"Which leaves TopDog," Sam said.

"TopDog? I bet that's who did it. The name is too good for the no-good scoundrel who set you up, David!" Wishbone sniffed at the empty tabletop. "Am I the only one here who's hungry?"

"I told the club members about the loophole in DynameX," David said. "TopDog could have used DynameX to get remote-control access to a bank computer. Once inside, he somehow got hold of one or several accounts and transferred their money to his bank account."

Sam held up a hand, frowning. "Wait a sec. I'm sure even a bank employee has to use a password to transfer money," she said. "How would TopDog get that?"

"That's another part of the puzzle I'm not sure of," David admitted. "But TopDog must have found a way."

Wishbone saw the curious glance Joe shot at David. "Why didn't you tell the F.B.I. agents about TopDog?" Joe asked. "If TopDog did set you up, shouldn't the F.B.I. know that?"

"I want to find out more on my own before I go to the F.B.I.," David answered. "But I don't even know TopDog's real name."

"Let us know how Joe and I can help you," Sam offered.

"And the dog!" Wishbone said. "You can count on me, David!" He pawed Joe's arm and looked up at him. "So, what's our plan, guys?"

"What about the other kids in the Computer Club? Couldn't they help, too?" Joe suggested.

David gave a nod, drumming his fingers on the table. "I want to talk to them about what happened. And I need to go on-line to see if I can track down TopDog."

"We terriers are experts at tracking. I'll help you sniff out that culprit and get Oakdale off the F.B.I.'s list of criminal hot spots—just as soon as I sniff out some pizza. Sam, can you help me out, please . . . ?"

David gazed across the booth at Sam and Joe. "It looks as if I've landed in the middle of a conspiracy, after all, guys," he said.

"I guess you have more in common with that guy from *The Thirty-Nine Steps* than we thought," Sam said.

"Richard Hannay," Joe said.

"And now the F.B.I. is after me," David said, "just like the way the British police went after Hannay when the underground political group known as the Black Stone set him up." He shook his head, thinking it over. "It's so unfair."

Suddenly, David was aware of the minutes ticking by, one after the other.

"I've got just two days to prove I'm innocent," David said. "I can't waste any time."

He jumped to his feet. "I bet some kids from the Computer Club are still at school," he told his friends.

"I'll go with you," Joe offered, but David shook his head.

"There isn't really anything you can do," he said. "Could you just call my parents and let them know where I am?"

Joe nodded. "Sure, David."

David glanced at his watch. It was five-thirty, already close to dinnertime. He hoped he wasn't too late. Somehow, he had to find out more about TopDog.

Fifteen minutes later, he pulled open the front door to Wilson High. He raced through the halls to the computer lab. He pushed the door to the room so hard that it hit the wall with a bang. Gilbert and Joanna—the only people still in the lab—both looked up in surprise.

"David! Just the person we were looking for," Gilbert said. "We wanted to talk to you about DynameX."

"You were right about that loophole," Joanna began. She broke off talking and stared at David. "Are you all right?"

David shook his head. "Some F.B.I. agents just paid me a surprise visit at my house. They think I hacked into a bank computer and stole a hundred thousand dollars."

"Very funny," said Gilbert.

"I'm serious," David said.

He sat down in front of the terminal next to Joanna and told her and Gilbert about the F.B.I.'s search of his room and the possibility of his arrest.

"I only have two days to prove I didn't do it," David finished.

Joanna had listened to the whole story in silence. Now she looked thoughtfully at David. "Didn't you once say you got into trouble with the F.B.I. before?" she asked.

"Yeah. It *was* an accident. And I *was* innocent, plus I helped the F.B.I. catch the bad guys. But I probably look suspicious because the last time they came to my house it had to do with an illegal transfer of money also," David said. "It's going to be pretty tough to prove I was set up by TopDog."

"TopDog?" Gilbert echoed.

David saw the surprised expressions that Gilbert and Joanna both shot at him. He explained his theory that TopDog had used the loophole in DynameX to hack into the bank's computer system, then set up David by using his signature.

"I mean, think about it," David went on. "He gave us two challenges that involved getting into other computers. I think he was planning to take that money all along. But I'm going to need help proving it."

David turned to the monitor in front of him and clicked on the Internet icon. It took him a few seconds to realize that Joanna and Gilbert hadn't moved or said a word. When he turned back around, he saw doubt on their faces.

"Come on, guys," David said. "You don't really think I stole that money. . . ."

"Well . . . you *did* get into trouble with the F.B.I. that other time," Gilbert said slowly.

"You said yourself that you like pushing a chal-

47

lenge to the limit," Joanna added. "And you were the one who discovered that loophole in DynameX."

David looked from one face to the other. He couldn't believe it. Gilbert and Joanna actually thought he could be the hacker.

*If even Joanna and Gilbert think I'm guilty,* he thought, *how am I going to convince the F.B.I. that I'm not?*

# Chapter Four

David leaned back against the couch in his living room later that evening. His parents were just saying good-bye to Mr. Lobel, the lawyer they had hired. David was glad Emily was upstairs watching a video. He wasn't certain if he or his parents could clearly explain his situation to a seven-year-old. The less she knew about this matter, the better.

The meeting had gone pretty well, David thought. His parents were both smiling as they closed the front door and came back into the living room.

"Mr. Lobel seems to think the F.B.I.'s case might not be as strong as the two agents are saying it is. It's very hard to trace this kind of electronic crime." David's father looked at David as he sat down in the armchair across from the couch. "That's some good news."

"Yeah," David agreed. As he replayed the meeting in his mind, he recalled that not all of the news had been good. "But if the F.B.I. thinks the evidence is

49

strong enough to take me to court, I could end up in a juvenile detention center. We could be fined thousands of dollars."

"That's not going to happen, David." His mother gave his shoulder an encouraging squeeze as she sat down next to him on the couch.

"Two days isn't a very long time, though," David said. "If I had more time, I'm sure I could figure out a way to clear myself. So far, I haven't had any luck."

David had tried a search of TopDog's name in the computer lab at school. He had even done an electronic search of TopDog's unique sign-off, "Blasting Off 4 Zondor." Neither search had turned up anything.

"You heard what Mr. Lobel said. He wants us to sit tight and leave everything to him," David's mother told him. "I think that's sound advice."

David shrugged, giving the sofa cushions a light punch. "I'm glad Mr. Lobel is helping, but . . . I can't just sit around doing nothing, while the F.B.I. is trying to put me in jail."

"Is David going to jail?" A small voice spoke up from the front hall.

David looked up to see Emily standing at the foot of the stairs in her Teddy bear nightgown. There was a scared look in her eyes.

"No one's going to jail," David's mother said.

As she got up and took Emily's hand to lead her back up the carpeted stairs, David stared after them. His mother's firm, soothing words echoed in his mind.

*No one's going to jail. . . .* If only he could be as sure as she was . . .

"You'd better call it a night." David's father's voice broke into David's thoughts. He must have seen the look in David's eyes, because he quickly added, "You need to get some rest so you can tackle this again tomorrow. Don't worry, son. Your mother and I know you haven't done anything wrong. We believe you and trust you. We're not going to let anything happen to you."

"Thanks, Dad."

David got up from the couch, said good-night, then went upstairs to his room. He knew his parents were there to support him, no matter what happened. But would that be enough this time?

David shook himself, pushing the thought from his mind. He got ready for bed, then settled in with the copy of *The Thirty-Nine Steps* that Joe had lent him. Within minutes, he was totally caught up in the story. Richard Hannay had fled to the English countryside. More than ever, David understood Hannay's urgent need to stay ahead of the police and the Black Stone. David was especially interested in a notebook Hannay had found, filled with coded notes. Hannay realized Scudder must have hidden it before he was murdered. He felt sure the notes would help him put an end to the Black Stone's plot to start a world war—if only he could succeed in decoding it.

"Too bad I don't have a coded notebook that could lead me to TopDog," David said to himself.

"David!" his mother called from downstairs. "Phone!"

David had been so caught up in his reading, he hadn't even heard the phone ring. Getting to his feet, he went to his parents' room and picked up the extension there. "Hello?"

"Hi, David."

David recognized Gilbert's voice. Maybe he had called to offer help. "What's up, Gilbert?" David asked.

"I talked to my uncle." Gilbert's voice came back over the line. "It looks like there's a problem with your working at that summer conference."

"Oh?" David asked. "What's the matter?"

"Well . . ." There was a long pause before Gilbert continued. He sounded embarrassed. "Everyone working at the conference has to have security clearance. Until you're cleared by the F.B.I., you're not eligible."

David felt as if a door had just slammed in his face. The door to his future. All because of TopDog.

Wishbone kept his eyes and ears alert as he trotted across the parking lot of the Royal Theater Friday morning. He crossed the street and continued for two blocks. He came to the patch of rhododendrons. The weathered clapboards of ToonTime Graphix were just coming into sight. "Here comes Commando Dog, ready for action and on the lookout for anything and anyone suspicious. . . ."

He paused and tilted his head slightly.

"That sounds like my buddies barking!"

Seconds later, the two younger greyhounds ran out from around the rear of the building. "Two out of three canines, present and accounted for." Wishbone barked his greeting, sniffing at the two dogs. "But where's Lightning?"

Both dogs danced nervously from paw to paw.

"Come on, guys. Don't you know where Lightning is?" Wishbone asked. Again, the two younger dogs just glanced this way and that with nervous eyes.

Looking at them, Wishbone felt the same chill that had gotten under his fur the last time he had been there. "Something tells me this is bad news. Where could the older greyhound be? Time for Commando Dog to move his mission inside."

Wishbone glanced upward, at the outside of ToonTime Graphix. Sunlight glinted off the windows. But Wishbone caught a flash of movement behind one of the upper panes. It was Hal Bolton, he realized. The

53

man was moving his hand while he talked on the phone in his loft office.

"I've sighted the enemy. Lightning had better be okay, Hal, or you'll have to answer to Commando Dog!"

Wishbone trotted to the sliding doors that led inside. Whoever had closed them last had left a small gap. Squeezing his muzzle into the crack, Wishbone was able to widen the opening enough to wiggle through.

"Yes! Now, if I can just find Lightning . . ."

As he trotted farther inside, Wishbone glanced cautiously around. The open work space was empty of people—and dogs. Hal was out of sight in the loft office. Wishbone didn't see Hal's employee, Corey, or Lightning, anywhere.

Wishbone trotted over to the kitchen area. On the floor next to the counter island were two food dishes and two water bowls.

He turned at the sound of nails clicking on the floor behind him. Lightning's two buddies had come inside and were looking at Wishbone curiously. "What happened, guys? Lightning is gone. And I don't think he took off with all his stuff on a canine backpacking trip."

Wishbone slowly circled the work space.

"There must be some clue to where he went. . . ."

The terrier sniffed at every plant, every piece of furniture, every huge machine.

"Lightning's scent is everywhere. What I need is something more. . . ."

He climbed up the metal staircase to the loft area. Steering clear of Hal's office, he trotted around the edge of the rest of the loft.

"No sign of him here, either. Which means—"

Wishbone stopped in mid-stride as the shadow of something large darkened the floor in front of him. He turned slowly to look behind him.

Hal Bolton stood in his office doorway. He stared down at Wishbone with anger in his eyes. Looking into those eyes, Wishbone felt every last bit of fur along his back stand up on end.

"What are you doing here, you little trouble-maker?" the man growled.

Then he lunged for Wishbone.

# Chapter Five

Wishbone jumped forward as fast as his four legs could carry him. A split-second later, Hal's hands swiped through the air where his tail had been.

"Hey! That's not detachable!" Wishbone shivered from his near escape. His paws slipped on the polished wood floor as he scrambled back around toward the stairs. "Time for Commando Dog to make a battle retreat."

"Oh, no, you don't . . ."

Wishbone heard Hal's muttering voice just before the man's brown shoes and khaki pants appeared in front of Wishbone's nose. "Uh-oh . . . Escape route's blocked!"

The terrier skidded to a stop on the slippery floor. Hal's red face loomed over him. His blond hair had fallen over his forehead. But it didn't hide the anger that burned in his eyes.

Wishbone yelped as Hal made another grab at him. "Yikes! No need to get rough, Hal . . ."

The terrier was panting as he turned and ran the other way. He heard Hal's shoes clomping on the floor right behind him. Wishbone's eyes were focused on an open doorway ahead. It offered the only possible escape. . . .

It wasn't until he saw a wooden desk just ahead of him that Wishbone realized where he was. "Hal's office. A dead end!"

Wishbone was moving fast. Just before his muzzle hit the desk, he managed to make a twisting jump up to Hal's chair. He scrambled onto the desktop, and his paws slipped on some papers, sending them flying in all directions.

"The Sport Tech project!" Hal grabbed at the falling papers as he raced into the office. "Why, you little . . ."

"Once and for all, I am *not* little, Hal! Just move aside, and Commando Dog will be out of here in a flash." As he tried to regain his balance, Wishbone knocked the telephone receiver from its cradle. His left hind paw pressed down on something hard and uncomfortable. "Ouch!"

He barked, and the sound echoed from the thing he was standing on.

"Surround sound?"

"You've turned on the speaker phone!" Hal said, tightly clutching the papers he'd gathered up from the floor. The words also echoed from the speaker—until Wishbone lifted his paw. Then the echo stopped.

Glancing down, Wishbone saw what he had been standing on: a white button that was part of a phone console at the edge of Hal's desk. As Wishbone backed away from it, he saw that Hal was closing in on him. He crouched down and let out a defensive growl.

"I'm sick of you dogs wrecking everything," Hal said. "Now . . . out!"

With his last word, Hal shot his hands out over the desk toward Wishbone.

"Hey!" Wishbone jumped the other way, back down onto the chair. He felt his hind legs knock against a cup, but he didn't turn or stop.

"My coffee . . ." Hal cried. "It's all over everything!"

Wishbone was already squeezing in between Hal's legs. Moving as fast as he could, he raced out of the office.

"Look at this mess. . . ." he heard Hal mutter.

Wishbone's nails tapped against the metal stairs as he flew down to the open work area below. The sound of Hal's voice, still grumbling inside the office, kept Wishbone's fur standing on end. At the foot of the stairs, the two younger greyhounds danced nervously from paw to paw.

"Don't worry, guys. I'm not giving up on you—or on Lightning. But for now . . ." Wishbone kept up the fast pace, heading for the sliding-glass doors. ". . . I'm outta here!"

He paused when he caught sight of the brown-haired young man who worked with Hal. He was walking up to the sliding-glass doors from the outside.

"Corey! You're just in time!" Wishbone cocked his head to the side, barking. "If you could just open that door a little wider. . . . Perfect!"

The young man stepped back, and Wishbone leaped through the opening. He looked back and saw Corey frowning at him. Wishbone could still hear Hal's loud voice coming from somewhere inside the building.

"Thanks!" Wishbone said, as he bounded onto the grassy lawn outside. "Commando Dog will have to continue his mission here later. 'Bye, guys!"

David was putting his books in his locker after his first class when Sam and Joe found him.

"Hi, David," Sam greeted him. She leaned against the locker next to David's, with her books tucked under her arm. "Joe and I were just talking. We really want to help you, David."

"We feel bad about you losing that internship with Gilbert's uncle," Joe said. "And about some of the kids in the Computer Club thinking you could be the hacker. There's *got* to be something we can do to prove to them that they are wrong."

David had called Sam and Joe twice the night before—once to tell them about what had happened in the computer lab, and a second time after Gilbert's phone call. "Knowing you guys are on my side is already a huge help," David told them. "Three heads are definitely better than one—especially since I have until tomorrow to prove to the F.B.I. that I'm not the hacker."

Sam shook her head slowly back and forth as

David grabbed his books for his next class and closed his locker door. "It isn't fair. Out of all the computer experts in the world, why did TopDog have to pick you to pin a crime on?" she asked.

"Beats me. I guess it's . . ." David stopped in mid-sentence as Sam's words sank in. "That's it!"

Sam traded puzzled glances with Joe. "What's it, David?" she asked.

"Well . . . what if I wasn't the only one?" David said. "I mean, maybe TopDog has been communicating with other computer clubs, too."

"Makes sense," Joe said, nodding as he shifted his weight from one foot to the other. "And if that's what TopDog did . . ."

"Then I have another way of tracking him down through other clubs!" David felt as if someone had just fired a shot to start a race. He didn't want to lose a second. "I've got to get on this right away. Thanks, guys!"

He started jogging down the hall toward the computer lab, but he stopped to glance over his shoulder at his friends.

"Meet me in the cafeteria at lunch, okay?" David called out.

"Sure," Joe called back. "Good luck, David!"

Adrenaline pumped through David as he made his way through the halls.

"What's the rush, David?" a voice spoke up, as David raced into the computer lab. "Got an F.B.I. surveillance team tailing you?"

David stopped short and turned toward the

voice. It was Shawn, sitting at a terminal at the front of the lab. He had on blue jeans and a green shirt. He let out a whistle as he turned toward David. "I heard you've got the feds after you. I'm really impressed," he said.

Half a dozen other people were in the lab, including Joanna and Elena. Every single one of them turned to stare at David.

David ignored them and hurried to the back of the room. *Obviously, Joanna and Gilbert have spread the word about the F.B.I. investigation.* David would have liked not to have the extra attention. He sat down at a terminal and logged on to the Internet.

He clicked on the icon to perform a search of the words "High School Computer Clubs." A long list of matches came up on his screen. As he scrolled down the list, David forgot all about Shawn and the other kids. He was completely focused on the names in front of him. *If I were TopDog,* he wondered, *which clubs would I choose? . . .*

For the next half-hour, David picked schools at random and logged on to each site. He sent e-mails and struck up conversations with people in computer club chat rooms. He tried every angle he could think of— mentioning TopDog, computer challenges, or any on-line contact from people outside the school computer club. So far, no luck.

"Okay . . ." David checked his watch as he logged off yet another Web site. There were five more minutes until the end of the period. Then he had to go to algebra class. "Just enough time for one more . . ."

David clicked on the next name.

"Riverside High Computer Club," he said. According to the listing, it was located in a town called Riverside, far away from Oakdale.

David touched the keyboard and mouse with the same strong determination he'd felt from the moment he'd awakened that morning. Moments later, he was logged on to the club's chat room. Just one other user was already visiting the site.

"Blondie, huh?" David said. He leaned forward to type a greeting.

Before his fingers reached the keys, a message from Blondie typed itself out on his screen: NICE NAME, BB. U R TALKING TO AN EXPERT ON BIG BROTHERS, SINCE I HAVE 3! PLEASE TELL ME U R NOT ONE OF THEM.

David smiled as he typed: NEGATIVE. Y WOULD THEY CHECK UP ON U?

Blondie's answer appeared right away: THE ON-LINE POLICE. MY PARENTS THINK I SPEND TOO MUCH TIME ON THE NET.

David laughed to himself when he saw Blondie's answer. His fingers flew over the keyboard as he typed his next comment: I KNOW HOW THAT IS. SO MANY COMPUTER GAMES . . . SO LITTLE TIME . . . DO U LIKE 2 TEST YOURSELF WITH CHALLENGES?

David wasn't sure where this conversation would go. At least he and Blondie were connecting.

U MUST B A MIND-READER! SECOND TIME THIS WEEK SOMEONE HAS APPROACHED ME ON-LINE ABOUT CHALLENGES.

As David read the words he jolted to super-alertness.

He typed out: SOMEONE HAS BEEN VISITING OUR COMPUTER CLUB CHAT ROOM, TOO! COULD B SAME PERSON. WHAT'S THE NAME?

David felt his entire body stiffen with anticipation. "Please," he said under his breath, as he stared at the screen. "Let it be . . ."

He broke off in mid-sentence as Blondie's answer appeared: DOES "TOPDOG" MEAN ANYTHING 2 U?

David could hardly believe his eyes. "Yes!" he cried, slapping his palm down next to the keyboard.

"Shh!" someone hissed.

David was so caught up in his investigation that he didn't even turn around. He typed: DEFINITELY!

Glancing to the left of the screen, he saw that someone with the code name "Ranger" had logged on to the Riverside chat room.

*Probably someone else from Riverside High's Computer Club,* he thought.

He typed: HI, RANGER. U KNOW TOPDOG, TOO?

Ranger didn't answer. Moments later, the name disappeared from the list of chat-room users.

David wasn't going to worry about it. He had to find out everything Blondie knew about TopDog. His fingers tapped on the computer keys as he wrote his next message: SOMETHING BIG GOING ON. I THINK TD IS INVOLVED. CAN U TELL ME

David touched the keys to complete his sentence, but . . . "Nothing!"

His computer had frozen!

He hit the controls that would re-boot the computer, but the screen remained frozen.

In the next instant, the chat room was replaced by a message that blinked in capital letters: CRITICAL ERROR!

"Don't tell me . . ."

David pressed hard on the keys that would re-boot his computer. As if he could somehow force the computer to work . . .

The screen went completely blank. David tried desperately to undo the error, but nothing he did made any difference.

"Oh, no!" Joanna's horrified voice came from across the lab. "My computer just crashed!"

"Mine, too," said a boy sitting next to David.

"No way!" David jumped up to look at the next terminal. It was blank. So was the next, and the next. . . . "The whole system has crashed!"

# Chapter Six

David stared in disbelief at the blank computer screens that lined the computer lab. "What is going on!" he cried.

Around him, the computer lab broke out into chaos. Kids jumped from their chairs or banged on their keyboards. Cries of frustration echoed through the room.

David ran back to his terminal and began typing in commands. "There's got to be a way to get the system up and running again," he muttered.

"Someone check the outlets! Or the breaker switches!" cried a brown-haired girl David didn't know.

"The power is still on," David heard Shawn say. "Something else must have made the system crash."

"Or *someone*," Joanna added.

Something in her voice made David turn around. Joanna was looking right at him. Her eyes were filled with doubt as she walked across the room toward him. She crossed her arms over the front of her shirt and said, "What do you think happened, David?"

"I don't know," he said. "All I know is that I got a message of 'critical error,' and then the system crashed."

"The computers were working fine before you logged on," Shawn said, coming to stand next to Joanna. "You sure have bad luck with computers lately."

David saw some of the other kids stop what they were doing to look at him. "Well, I didn't make the computers crash," he said.

"Maybe you didn't," Joanna said, her eyes showing some sign of doubt. "But with this whole F.B.I. thing . . . We can't rule it out, that's all."

David couldn't believe what he was hearing. There had to be a way to get Joanna and the other kids to understand. But the way they were looking at him, he felt as if the word *guilty* were stamped across his chest.

*This is how Richard Hannay must have felt when people treated him like a criminal,* thought David. All David wanted to do was straighten everything out. But it seemed the harder he tried, the more twisted the whole situation became.

"Boy, am I glad to see you guys," David said an hour later, as he reached the cafeteria table where Sam and Joe were sitting. "You're not going to believe what happened."

They both looked up from their sandwiches and milk. "What?" asked Sam.

"Did you find any other computer clubs that Top-Dog contacted?" Joe spoke up at the same time.

"Yes." David sat down at the table. While he unwrapped his roast-beef sandwich and opened his carton of milk, he told Sam and Joe all that had happened in the computer lab.

"So now everyone in the lab thinks *you* made the computers crash?" Sam said, shaking her head in disbelief.

"Too bad you didn't even get to finish talking to Blondie," Joe said.

"That's the part that's really frustrating," David said. "I'm going to try calling her at her school. But it's in a town called Riverside, and it's long distance. Do you two have any change?"

Sam reached into the front pocket of her backpack, which rested on the floor next to their table. "Here," she said, pulling out a calling card. "My dad gave this to me for emergencies. I'd say this qualifies."

"Thanks, Sam."

David ate his lunch so fast he barely tasted it. He, Sam, and Joe tossed their trash into the bins near the door. Then they headed for the pay phones outside the administration office.

As they walked, David noticed that Joe was looking down at his sneakers. Finally, Joe looked at David and said, "Don't you think there's something weird about what happened? I mean, the way the computers crashed right when you found Blondie . . ."

"It can't be a coincidence. I've been thinking about that, too," David said. "TopDog must have made it happen. Someone else logged on to the chat room while Blondie and I were talking. Right after that, things went haywire. . . ."

"So the computers crashed just as you were about to find out something important," Sam finished. Her blue eyes shone with excitement as she stopped next to a pay phone and lifted the receiver from its cradle. "You've *got* to reach Blondie."

David dialed Information and got the telephone number of Riverside High School. Then Sam punched in the code from her calling card. Moments later, David gripped the receiver and listened to the rings. After the second one, someone picked up.

"Riverside High School." A woman's voice came over the line. "How may I help you?"

"I'm trying to reach someone in the Computer Club," David said. "I don't know her real name, but she uses the code name 'Blondie' on the Internet."

There was a pause before the woman spoke again. "I'm sorry, but there isn't a phone in the computer lab," she told David.

"Then could you give me the names of the kids in the Computer Club?" David asked. He motioned to Sam and Joe to give him something to write with.

"No, I cannot do that," the woman said. "It's our

school policy never to give out student names over the phone."

David's fingers clamped down on the pen Joe had handed him. "Please," he said into the receiver. "It's really important."

"If you'll leave me your name and telephone number, I'll post it in the computer lab. I'm afraid that's all I can do for you," the woman said.

*It's not enough!* David wanted to shout. But he knew the woman was doing all she could to help him.

"Thanks. I'd appreciate it," he told her. "My name is David, but Blondie knows me as BigBrother. Could you leave a message for Blondie to call BigBrother as soon as possible?"

He gave the woman his phone number, thanked her again, then hung up.

"You couldn't get through?" Sam guessed. She leaned against the wall next to the pay phone, twisting a strand of blond hair in her fingers.

David shook his head and explained. "I'll have to wait until she calls back . . . unless I can find another way to go on-line."

They had already taken a few steps down the hall when Joe snapped his fingers. "The Henderson Memorial Public Library!" he said. "It has at least one computer that's hooked up to the Internet. We could go after school."

"Okay," David agreed. "I promised my parents I'd check in with them at home. They're meeting with the lawyer again today. But I could go right after that. Is your mom working today?"

Joe's mother was the research librarian at the library. "She'll be there until eight," Joe said, nodding. "I'll call her and make sure the system is up and running. Sam and I will wait for you at my house, okay?"

"Sounds good," David agreed. He was glad to be doing all he could to prove his innocence. But as he, Sam, and Joe headed for their next classes, David was very aware that time was running out.

Tomorrow, the F.B.I. agents could be back to arrest him.

David lay on the couch with his copy of *The Thirty-Nine Steps* after school. He'd come home to find that his parents hadn't yet returned from the lawyer's office. While he waited for them, he decided he might as well find out what happened next to Richard Hannay.

It didn't take long before he was really into the story. David could practically feel the fear that ran through Hannay when he realized a small plane was tracking him from the skies above, while a car searched for him on the roads. As Hannay looked for cover in the open countryside, David knew the Black Stone would kill Hannay if it caught up to him. Even when Hannay found temporary safety in an isolated country inn, David felt that danger was nearby.

David read on, while Hannay tried to find the key to understanding the coded notes in Franklin Scudder's notebook. It was exactly the kind of challenge that David enjoyed tackling. He understood all of the frustration Hannay felt when he kept coming across a phrase that he simply could not make any sense of: "39 steps."

*It's almost as bad as "Blasting Off 4 Zondor." I don't know what that means, either,* thought David. *If I could just make some sense of it all, I might be able to—*

"Hi, David. We're back."

David blinked at the sound of his mother's voice. It was a surprise to look up and find himself in his living room, instead of in the British countryside. But there were his parents, smiling at him as they walked in from the front hall.

"Hi, Mom. Hi, Dad." David closed his book and sat up to make room for them on the couch. "What did Mr. Lobel say?"

His dad loosened his tie, then clapped an arm around David's shoulders as he sat down next to him. "Mr. Lobel and his partners are doing everything they can. They could use your help."

"David, is there anything else that you've thought of that might help?" his mother added, sitting down on his other side.

David took a deep breath, relieved to have his parents beside him. "Mom, Dad, something really weird happened at school today. I think Mr. Lobel should know about it. . . ."

He told his parents about finding Blondie on-line, and about the computers crashing. Frowns appeared on their faces as he told them his guess that TopDog was responsible.

"I'm sure Blondie will call you back as soon as she gets your message," his mother said.

"At least a telephone line is private," his father added. "TopDog won't be able to eavesdrop or make the line go dead."

David frowned as he ran his dad's words through his mind. "Privacy . . ." he said slowly. "A person's privacy is a good thing, I guess. But sometimes . . ." He shrugged, letting his voice trail off.

David's mom turned to him with a surprised look on her face. "You're not so sure?"

"TopDog is hiding behind the privacy of the In-

73

ternet," David explained. "TopDog used the secrecy of the Web to commit a major crime and set me up."

"Well, TopDog is not going to get away with it," his dad said firmly. "Your mother and I—and Mr. Lobel and his partners—are going to make sure of that."

David nodded, feeling a fresh wave of courage wash over him. Richard Hannay had found himself in an even tougher situation. Yet Hannay never lost his nerve—or his determination to outsmart the Black Stone. *Hannay sure has guts,* thought David. *He keeps his head. I guess that's what I need to do, too.*

"I'm going to make sure TopDog doesn't get away, too," David said. "You can bet on it."

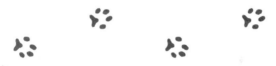

Wishbone awoke from his afternoon nap to hear his best buddy's footsteps in the front hall.

"Joe!"

Wishbone stretched, then jumped down from the big red chair in the study. He had a mission. The terrier felt refreshed—and ready to continue his search for Lightning. Tail wagging, he trotted to the front hall, where Joe and Sam were putting down their backpacks.

"Red alert, guys! Lightning is missing again, and . . ."

"Let's call your mom and make sure David can go on-line on one of the computers at the library," Sam said. As she spoke, she leaned down to pet Wishbone.

"Hi, Wishbone," Joe said without really paying the dog much attention. Then he turned back to Sam.

"I really hope Blondie knows something that can help David track down TopDog," he said.

Wishbone sat back on his haunches and stared up at his friends. "Isn't anyone listening?" Then he took a closer look at his friends' faces. They needed his help. "You need tracking? I'm your dog! Give me something to sniff, and I'll be on the trail!"

He followed at his pals' heels as Joe and Sam went into the kitchen. Joe reached for the phone, then paused with his hand on the handset.

"There's a message," he said, gazing at the red light on the machine.

Wishbone barked as Joe pressed a button on the machine. "It's Hal! Don't believe a word he says, Joe!"

Wishbone had heard the message when it was recorded earlier. But the sound of Hal's voice being played back on the machine still made his fur stand on end.

"This is Hal Bolton, of ToonTime Graphix . . ."

As Hal described the mess Wishbone had made of the ToonTime Graphix office that morning, Joe's face grew more serious.

". . . your dog has caused enough damage," Hal's recorded voice said. "I'd appreciate it if you would keep him away from my office from now on."

"Wishbone . . ." Joe aimed a warning glance down at him. "This is not like you. How could you do that, boy?"

"It's not like it sounds. I was looking out for Lightning and his buddies!" Wishbone insisted. "Something is going on over there. And it's not good, Joe!"

Joe reached out for Wishbone's leash, on its hook next to the kitchen door. "We're going over there right now to apologize for the mess you made," he said.

"I'll help you clean up, if we need to," Sam said.

"Thanks," Joe said.

"Hal is the one who should apologize!" Wishbone said firmly.

Joe and Sam were distracted by the sound of the front doorbell and didn't seem to hear the dog.

"That must be David," Sam said, turning away from Wishbone. "He can ride with us until we reach Oak Street. Then we'll split up. We'll go to ToonTime Graphix, and he'll head to the library."

A few minutes later, Wishbone was running alongside his friends' bikes as they rode in the direction of town. The autumn breeze ruffled his fur. The pavement was cool and hard beneath his paws. As he ran, the terrier searched out the surrounding lawns and woods with his eyes.

"No Lightning here . . . or there . . ."

Wishbone sniffed around the driveway of the post office, at the corner of Oak Street. Dogs loved the old stump next to the flagpole. But today . . .

"No Lightning there, either."

David slowed his bike at Oak Street and looked at Sam and Joe. "Here's where I turn off, guys," he said.

"'Bye, David. Good luck!" Wishbone barked his farewell, then trotted across the street.

The terrier had already reached the far side when his paws froze on the sidewalk. Some yards up ahead, an animal was lying at the side of the road.

"Guys! It's a dog!"

Even from a distance, Wishbone could see that it was in trouble.

"This way . . . quick!" Wishbone raced forward, barking his alarm. As he approached the dog, he picked up Lightning's familiar scent. Wishbone eagerly sniffed all over the greyhound's brown fur and white-flecked muzzle.

It was his buddy, all right. Lightning's fur was matted and caked with a sticky black goo that made Wishbone's nose itch. Wishbone stood over his friend and barked loudly.

"Lightning! Wake up, buddy!"

The greyhound lay motionless, his eyes tightly closed.

# Chapter Seven

David had just turned down Oak Street when Wishbone's constant barking made him look back over his shoulder. The terrier was standing over a dark shape at the side of the road. David squinted, but he couldn't see it clearly.

"It's Lightning!" he heard Sam exclaim.

In a flash, David turned his bike around. Sam and Joe had already dropped their bikes at the side of the road and were bent over the greyhound. As David rode up to them, he saw Lightning's grimy brown fur, closed eyes, and very still body. "Is he . . . ?"

"He's alive." Joe pointed to the dog's rib cage, which rose and fell with his rapid, shallow breathing. "He looks like he's in bad shape, though. ToonTime Graphix is right up the road. We'd better take him there right away. I'll carry him."

Wishbone barked, licking Lightning's muzzle and ears. David was glad to see the greyhound finally open

78

his eyes. Lightning thumped his tail weakly against the pavement. He shifted his head slightly before closing his eyes.

"Let's leave our bikes here until we get back," David said.

He still wanted to get to the library, so he could try to reach Blondie again on-line. But he could see that Lightning needed to be cared for right away.

Joe carried the greyhound up the road, and Wishbone trotted alongside. He kept his muzzle in the air, sniffing the greyhound.

"He looks really tired," Sam said, walking beside Joe. "Look how dirty his coat is. And his paws . . . they've got bits of asphalt all over them."

As they walked, David stared at the sticky black smudge the asphalt had left on Sam's fingers. "He looks like he's traveled somewhere really far."

"They're resurfacing the main highway, but that's way out of town," Joe said. He frowned, shifting Lightning's weight in his arms. "Mr. Bolton must be worried sick about you, boy."

All of a sudden, Wishbone let out a stream of rapid-fire barks, and he pawed nonstop at Joe's legs. The sounds were so urgent-sounding that David had the feeling Wishbone was trying to tell them something very important.

"Down, boy," Joe said, struggling to keep his balance.

David was relieved some ten minutes later when Joe pointed out the weathered, converted barn where

79

ToonTime Graphix was located. As the group approached the sliding-glass doors that led inside, Joe handed Lightning over to David. He reached into his back pocket, pulled out Wishbone's leash, and clipped it to the terrier's collar.

"Sorry, boy," he said. "I can't take any chances after what happened with you here this morning. You can go in, but you have to behave."

As they stepped inside, David looked around the big, open work space with a loft office above. Two men were working at what looked like high-tech computers in the main work area.

"There's Mr. Bolton and Corey Anderson," Joe said.

When they saw Lightning, both men stopped what they were doing.

"Lightning!" the older man exclaimed. He looked surprised. His blond hair fell over his forehead as he rushed over. He glanced at Joe, Sam, David, and Wishbone. "Where did you find him this time?" he asked, a confused frown wrinkling his forehead.

"I got your message about Wishbone, Mr. Bolton," Joe explained. "We were on our way over to apologize when we found Lightning."

Mr. Bolton had been staring down angrily at Wishbone, but he snapped out of it. Taking Lightning in his arms, he called over his shoulder, "Corey! Get a blanket."

The younger man still sat at his computer, a few yards away. As David glanced over, the image of a brightly colored spaceship shooting across Corey's monitor immediately caught his attention. It looked like a futuristic cartoon with exaggerated shapes, quirky lines, and intense, vivid colors.

As Mr. Bolton approached with Lightning, Corey clicked his mouse button and the spaceship disappeared from the screen, replaced by a three-dimensional chart. "Sure, Mr. Bolton," Corey said, jumping up.

The next few minutes passed in a blur. Wishbone kept getting in the way while Corey and Mr. Bolton settled Lightning on a couch near the kitchen area. Every time Mr. Bolton got near the old dog, Wishbone growled at the man. Joe kept apologizing, but Wishbone didn't let up.

"Stop it, Wishbone!" Joe said, tugging on Wishbone's leash. "Sorry, Mr. Bolton. He doesn't usually behave like this."

David turned as two younger greyhounds came bounding through the opened sliding-glass doors. They ran over to Lightning and sniffed him all over. Mr. Bolton barely seemed to notice them. He looked as if he were trying to keep his temper as he set down a bowl of water next to Lightning.

"Look, I appreciate your bringing Lightning back," he told Joe. "I must have left the doors open. I was starting to think I'd never see him again. Thanks . . ." Mr. Bolton pushed his hair off his forehead with an impatient swipe of his hand. "Could you take your dog home now? I think Lightning needs to rest. He'll be fine once he gets some food."

The old greyhound did seem to be acting more

alert, David noticed. He lapped at the water Mr. Bolton had brought him. He wagged his tail steadily. His eyes were clearer as they followed the activity around him. One ear lifted when the telephone rang.

"It's for you, Mr. Bolton," Corey called a moment later, cupping his hand over the receiver.

Mr. Bolton nodded. "I'll take it in my office, Corey," he said. He walked toward the stairs that led up to the loft area, then paused with his hand on the railing. "Thanks again for bringing Lightning back, Joe."

*The man was polite enough,* David thought. *But he sure is eager to get us out of ToonTime Graphix.*

"No problem," Joe said. Then they all said good-bye and headed for the doors.

Corey was already back at his computer. The 3-D chart was gone, and once again the spaceship streaked across the screen. "Cool graphics," David commented, stopping next to Corey.

"Thanks," Corey said, with a wide grin.

"Wow!" Sam gave an impressed nod as she and Joe looked, too. "Did you do that?"

Corey nodded. Lowering his voice, he added, "This job is only temporary. As soon as I get together enough money to start my own computer company, I'm gone."

He shot a quick glance at Mr. Bolton, talking on the phone in the loft office.

"Check this out," Corey said. He tapped a few keys on his keyboard. The spaceship hurtled past meteors and asteroids, on a collision course with a rocket that came into view in the distance.

"This is right up your alley, David," Joe said. He gave Wishbone's leash a gentle tug, to keep the terrier from pulling him back toward Lightning.

"You like computers?" Corey asked.

"He sure does," Sam answered. "David is a computer genius and is the most dedicated member of the Wilson High Computer Club. He spends a lot of time on the Internet."

"I used to, anyway," David added. "When I still had a computer . . ."

Corey turned his head around to look at David, suddenly very curious. "What happened to your computer?"

"It's a long story," David said.

All of a sudden, Mr. Bolton's voice boomed out from above. "Get back to work, Corey."

David looked up to see the older man standing next to the stairs. He frowned down at them from the loft. Wishbone let out a growling, threatening bark, straining against his leash.

"I have to go out for a while," Mr. Bolton said to Corey. "I want you to have those charts ready when I get back."

David turned back to Corey and was surprised to see the sci-fi animation replaced by charts and graphs.

"No problem, Mr. Bolton," Corey said, smiling up at the other man.

"We'd better go, guys," Joe said, pulling Wishbone toward the sliding-glass doors.

David followed Sam and Joe out into the evening.

It was a relief to be outside in the fresh air. As they headed for the road, David tried to shake off the uncomfortable feeling that had come over him while they were inside. "Did anyone else get the feeling that Corey wasn't supposed to be working on that animation project during office hours?"

Joe shrugged. "I'm just happy to get Wishbone out of there," he said.

"I don't think I've ever seen Wishbone like that before," Sam said. She reached down to scratch the terrier behind his ears, then smiled at Joe and David. "At least Lightning is back where he belongs."

Wishbone pulled against his leash, trying to lead Joe back to ToonTime Graphix. "I don't want to leave Lightning and his pals with Hal. Don't you see what's happening? Hal is trying to get rid of Lightning!"

Wishbone didn't think he could make his point any more strongly. Yet Joe, Sam, and David kept walking toward the road. Wishbone had no choice but to follow.

He sighed as he trotted alongside them. "No one ever listens to the dog."

The sun was sinking behind the treetops. Wishbone padded across the pavement. He heard birds chirping in the nearby trees, but the darkening twilight hid them from view. Glancing up at David, Wishbone saw the boy squint at his watch.

"It's almost six-thirty. I'd better get over to the

library," David said. As he walked forward, Wishbone saw the determined set to his jaw.

"Excellent idea!" Wishbone pulled against his leash, looking up at his best buddy. "How about lifting the temporary restraining order on the cute little dog, Joe? I'd like to—"

At that moment, Wishbone heard the sound of a car coming up behind them. He cocked his head around curiously. The car was just a dark blur on the road behind them.

"What? No lights?" Wishbone felt a sudden chill as he watched the shape move closer. "You're moving a little fast, pal. . . . Hey! Stay in the lane, or you're going to—"

The terrier yelped as the car swerved onto the shoulder, heading their way.

"Look out!" he barked.

Joe and Sam both turned at the same time. Wishbone saw the surprise—and fear—on their faces.

"David! Watch it!" Joe shouted, as he let go of Wishbone's leash and pushed Sam to the side.

David was a few steps ahead of them. He started to turn, but the car was moving so quickly. . . . All Wishbone saw was a flash of metallic blue.

And David was right in its path.

# Chapter Eight

"No!" David cried, his face frozen with fear.

Wishbone was already pushing off with his hind legs in a flying leap. As he flew toward David, Wishbone felt the heat of the car right on top of them. His canine senses were overwhelmed by the car's roaring engine and heat and fumes. . . .

"Ooomph!" Wishbone hit David's hip with the full force of his front paws.

As he and David tumbled to the grass off the side of the road, Wishbone heard Sam scream. A split-second later, the blue car zoomed past so close that it created a wind that whipped at Wishbone's fur.

Wishbone panted as he got up and ran back to David. "Talk about a close call!" He licked at David's hands and face. "Looks like all the parts are still in working order. . . ."

David slowly pushed himself to a sitting position. He wore a stunned expression on his face. "Wh-what happened?" he asked.

"David! Are you all right?" Sam cried as she raced over.

Joe was right behind her. "That was a metallic-blue sports car. I recognized that model. It's a Stinger. Didn't the driver see us?" he asked, his brown eyes focused on the road ahead of them. Suddenly, he blinked in surprise. "Hey! The license plate is covered up. . . ."

Wishbone turned just in time to see the flashy-looking sports car screech around a corner. Then it vanished. As the sound of the engine faded, David got slowly to his feet.

"I'm fine, guys," he said, brushing dirt and gravel off his hands. "Nice save, Wishbone. Thanks."

"All in the canine line of duty." Wishbone wagged his tail. He was glad David was all right. Still . . . "Something's not right here, guys."

David seemed to share the terrier's concern. Wishbone saw that the boy was frowning in the direction in which the blue sports car had gone. "This is spooky," said David. "Why would someone cover up a license plate? Or not turn on their headlights when it's practically dark? You guys don't think . . ."

"You think the driver *tried* to hit you?" Sam asked, her eyes opening wide.

"It sure seemed like that." David frowned and kicked at the pavement with his sneaker. "He might have just been trying to scare me. But if that was Top-Dog, it means he's discovered my real identity!"

"But you're just a name on a computer screen to TopDog," Joe said, as he bent down to unclip Wishbone's collar. "How could TopDog find you in real life?"

David shoved his hands in his pockets as he thought it over. "Beats me," he said. "The Computer Club Web site gives the name of our town. But I'm sure TopDog could never find out my real name on-line." Wishbone saw the almost unnoticeable shiver that shook David. "If TopDog knows who I am . . ."

"Then you could be in real danger, David," Sam finished. "That means it's more important than ever for you to talk to Blondie and find out what she knows about TopDog."

David looked at his watch and started walking faster. "It's already six-forty-five," he said. "The library's only open for another hour and fifteen minutes."

"We'll go with you," Joe said.

In a matter of minutes, they reached the corner of Oak Street. Sam, Joe, and David got their bikes from the side of the road and strapped on their helmets. As they began riding down Oak Street toward the library, Wishbone ran to keep up with them.

The terrier caught a strong whiff of pepperoni and garlic as they passed Pepper Pete's Pizza Parlor. Moments later, he heard a familiar voice call out from behind them.

"David!"

Wishbone turned, then barked a greeting to Sam's father, Walter Kepler. "Hi, Walter! The garlic twists smell extra good this evening!"

Sam's father waved from the doorway of Pepper Pete's. Looking back over his haunches, Wishbone saw David, Sam, and Joe circle their bikes around and ride back.

"I'm glad I saw you," Walter told them. "Your mother just called looking for you, David. She said to tell you someone tried to reach you at home. A girl named . . ."

"Blondie?" David guessed.

Walter pulled a scrap of paper from his apron pocket. "Yes, that's it," he said with a nod. "Blondie. She said to call her back at this number."

"Thanks, Mr. Kepler." David took the piece of paper, then turned to Sam and Joe. "I'll call right away."

Sam was already parking her bike in front of Pepper Pete's. "Here, David," she said, reaching into the front pocket of her backpack. "Use my calling card."

Wishbone sniffed at the plastic card she pulled out. David thanked her and took it, then headed inside Pepper Pete's with the kind of eagerness Wishbone usually showed for Ellen's ginger-snap treats.

"This could be really important," David said.

Wishbone wagged his tail as he trotted through the doorway in front of Joe and Sam. "We're right behind you, David!"

David took a deep breath and rang Gilbert's doorbell. Joe and Wishbone had gone home. Sam had stayed at Pepper Pete's to help her dad. It was eight-fifteen and it had been only an hour and a half since he had received the message from Blondie. But in that short time, David felt that his situation had definitely changed for the better.

The Pickerings' front door was opened by Gilbert.

"Hi, David. The other kids from the Computer Club—Joanna, Elena, and Shawn—are all here, just as you asked," Gilbert said. David could see the look of curiosity on the other boy's face as he stepped back to let David in. "What's this all about?"

"I've arranged for us to talk to someone from another high school's Computer Club. She's got information about the computer hacker."

David followed Gilbert upstairs to his room. Joanna was sitting on the chair in front of Gilbert's computer. Elena sat cross-legged on the bed, while Shawn looked over the titles on Gilbert's bookshelf.

Everyone's eyes zeroed in on David. David saw questioning looks written on all their faces.

"What's going on, David?" Joanna finally asked.

"There's someone I want you to talk to," he said. David unzipped his jacket and took it off, then hung it on the back of Gilbert's desk chair. "Her code name is 'Blondie.'"

"How did you find her?" Elena asked, leaning forward on the bed.

David held up a hand to stop the group from asking more questions. "She's waiting for us to log on to a chat room so she can tell you herself."

He saw that Gilbert had already logged on to the Internet. Leaning past Joanna, David typed the Web address of the TeenTalk chat room where he and Blondie had agreed to meet.

"Cool," he said, checking the list of users. "Blondie's already logged on."

Gilbert, Shawn, and Elena circled around as David reached in front of Joanna once more and typed: HI, BLONDIE. BB HERE. I'M WITH EVERYONE FROM THE WILSON HIGH SCHOOL COMPUTER CLUB. THEY WANT 2 HEAR WHAT U TOLD ME, OKAY?

Her answer appeared right away: OK, BB. HERE GOES. YOUR COMPUTER CLUB AND MINE HAVE SOMETHING IN COMMON. WE HAVE BOTH BEEN TALKING TO TOPDOG. I GUESS HE LIKES 2 SPREAD HIS CHALLENGES AROUND.

Joanna blinked in surprise at Gilbert's screen. She immediately reached out with her slender fingers and typed: TD GAVE CHALLENGES 2 YOUR CLUB, 2? WHAT KIND?

David could see that Blondie had gotten everyone's attention. Joanna, Shawn, Gilbert, and Elena stared wide-eyed at the screen.

Within a few moments, Blondie's answer typed itself out: FIRST CHALLENGE WAS FIGURING OUT HOW 2 MAKE ANOTHER COMPUTER CRASH. . . .

"Whoa!" Gilbert said under his breath.

"You think that's how our system crashed today?" Joanna asked the others.

Elena turned to David with puzzled eyes. "But why would TopDog do that?"

"Keep reading, guys," David said, nodding back at Gilbert's computer screen. "There's more."

Blondie's explanation went on: I WON THE CHALLENGE BY SENDING AN OVERLOAD OF DATA OVER CHANNELS THAT COULDN'T HANDLE IT. . . .

David knew that computer data was transmitted over different channels. Sending an overload of information over a channel that didn't have the capability of handling it would cause a system to crash.

WHEN I GAVE ANSWER 2 TD, TD SAID IT WOULD COME IN HANDY. SORRY, BB. IF I'D KNOWN WHAT WOULD HAPPEN, I NEVER WOULD HAVE TRIED THE CHALLENGE.

"But . . ." Shawn raked a hand through his wiry red hair, his eyes still glued to the computer screen. "What does this have to do with the computer hacking?"

Joanna typed out Shawn's question, then added some thoughts of her own: STILL DOESN'T PROVE TD IS THE HACKER. Y DO U SUSPECT TD?

Blondie's answer appeared right away: TD CRASHED YOUR SYSTEM WHEN I WAS ABOUT 2 TELL BB ABOUT ANOTHER CHALLENGE TD GAVE OUR CLUB—TO MONITOR SOMEONE ELSE'S COMPUTER AND RECORD EVERY KEYSTROKE

MADE. ONLY 1 KID COMPLETED CHALLENGE. POSTED THE RESULT ON OUR WEB SITE. . . .

"TopDog could have gotten the bank's password that way!" Gilbert said, smacking the palm of his hand against his head.

As David turned to look at the others, he could almost see the light bulb blink on above their heads.

"Oh, my gosh . . ." Joanna murmured. She quickly typed her next comment: SO TD MONITORS THE COMPUTER OF A BANK EMPLOYEE WHO KNOWS THE PASSWORD INTO THEIR CUSTOMER ACCOUNTS, AND THAT'S ALL IT TAKES. BANK WAVES GOOD-BYE 2 $100,000, AND TD GETS AWAY WITH IT. . . .

Blondie's answer was immediate: BINGO!

David saw a group of heads nod as the others read what Joanna and Blondie had typed out. *Finally,* he thought, *we're all on the same page!*

"And we're the ones who told TopDog how to do it!" Shawn said.

"I guess we were pretty foolish to be so trusting," Joanna added. Her fingers flew to the keyboard: WE TOLD TD HOW 2 GET REMOTE CONTROL ACCESS 2 ANOTHER COMPUTER. WE GAVE TD THE KNOW-HOW 2 COMMIT A MAJOR THEFT AND SET UP BB 2 TAKE THE BLAME! TD TRICKED US!

When Joanna was done, she tucked her hair behind her ears and turned to David.

"I feel really dumb, David," she said. "I never should have doubted you when you first told me Top-Dog was the hacker. Sorry."

"The important thing is that we're all on the same side now," David said.

He turned back to the computer monitor as Blondie's next comment typed itself out: WHAT DO WE DO NOW?

"That's the real question," David said, pointing at the message. "I mean, what do we—"

All of a sudden, the chat room was replaced by multicolored helixes that spiraled around the screen to form a rectangle.

"Hey! That's just like what you used on your surprise message, David," Gilbert said.

"Uh-oh." David felt something tighten in the pit of his stomach. "It must be TopDog. . . ."

A moment later, neon-green words spelled themselves out inside the rectangle: BACK OFF, DE-TECTIVES . . . OR NEXT TIME I WON'T MISS.

# Chapter Nine

David stared at the threatening message on Gilbert's monitor. He remembered the roaring engine and the searing heat coming from the tailpipe of the metallic-blue Stinger.

"'Next time I won't miss'. . . ." Elena turned to David with a puzzled frown. "What does that mean?"

David told her and others about the sports car that had nearly hit him earlier that evening. "Now I know it was TopDog," he said. "Somehow, TopDog knows who I am. And if he knows who I am, he must be local."

"That's really scary, David," Joanna said, shivering.

Gilbert pushed his round-framed glasses up onto the bridge of his nose. "Yes, but remember, now we know something about TopDog, too."

"Right. TopDog must live somewhere around Oakdale," said David.

"That's not a good thing." Shawn leaned back

96

against Gilbert's desk and crossed his arms over his chest. "You're in serious danger, David."

Now that David knew the others believed him, he was eager to do whatever had to be done to track down TopDog. He took a deep breath, looking from face to face. "If we all work together, I know we can outsmart TopDog. Are you all with me?"

Joanna, Gilbert, Elena, and Shawn exchanged quick glances before turning back to David.

"Yes," Joanna said, with a firm nod.

"Great!" David sat down on Gilbert's bed. As the others settled in around him, the feeling of excitement was almost electric. "Okay. We've got to come up with a plan. . . ."

Wishbone was curled up on the couch next to Joe after eating a late dinner, when the phone rang. He jumped up, barking, and sniffed at the portable telephone that lay on the coffee table. "Phone!"

"I've got it!" Joe called to his mom, who was in the kitchen. He reached over, grabbed the handset, and pressed the button to answer. "Hello?"

Joe listened, then sat up straighter.

"David?" he said into the receiver. "What happened at Gilbert's?"

Wishbone rested his paws on Joe's leg and looked up at his best buddy. "Don't leave the dog out of the loop, Joe! Joe . . . ?"

Joe didn't answer. He gripped the handset close to his ear, nodding as he listened. "Uh-huh . . . Wow! . . . Really?"

"What, Joe?" Wishbone pawed at Joe's leg. Looking back over his haunches, he saw Ellen step over to the doorway leading from the kitchen. "You look just as curious as I am, Ellen!"

"Sure, David," Joe said into the receiver. "Let me know if you need Sam and me to do anything. . . . Okay. Talk to you tomorrow. 'Bye."

He hung up the phone.

"Did David tell his parents about the sports car?" Ellen asked, with a worried look on her face.

"Yes. They reported the incident to the police," Joe said.

"Good. I'm glad to hear David wasn't hurt. All of you could have been injured," Ellen said.

"We'll be careful, Mom," Joe said. "Oh, the reason David called was to say that TopDog cut in when he and the other kids in the Computer Club were talking to Blondie."

"What are David and the other kids in the Computer Club planning to do?" Ellen asked, coming over to sit next to Wishbone and Joe.

"He and the rest of the Computer Club members are working together now to try to prove TopDog is the hacker," Joe said.

"Excellent!" Wishbone rolled over on his back and let Joe rub his belly. "Take it from a dog who knows—teamwork is the way to go!"

"I'm glad to hear that," Ellen said, leaning back against the sofa cushions.

"Some of the kids are going to keep trying to track down TopDog on their personal computers," Joe replied. "Gilbert called his uncle, too. Dr. Pickering has given his permission to David and Gilbert to let them use one of the high-tech, cutting-edge computers they've got at Littleton Aerospace. They're going over there tomorrow morning."

Wishbone wagged his tail as he gazed up at his best buddy. "Sounds like David isn't wasting any time in taking action. It's time for me to make my next move, too! While David is at Littleton Aerospace, Commando Dog will be out on a stealth mission at ToonTime Graphix. . . ."

David lay back on his bed, with *The Thirty-Nine Steps* propped against his bent legs. It was late, but David couldn't sleep. Once he started reading, he became more wide awake than ever.

No sooner did Richard Hannay make his getaway from the car and plane that were tracking him over the countryside than he found himself being chased on foot by the local police. Hannay thought he was safe when he found shelter in an old farmhouse. The owner seemed to be sympathetic to Hannay's plight—until Hannay discovered he was the leader of the Black Stone group!

The Black Stone leader locked Hannay in a storage room filled with explosives. Hannay used his engineering training to build a bomb and escape. Hannay reached the home of a government official who was willing to help him.

David heaved a sigh of relief when the government official told Hannay that he was no longer suspected by the police. "'I felt a free man once more,'" he read aloud, "'for I was now up against my country's enemies only, and not my country's law.'"

But Hannay's relief didn't last long. He discovered that the Black Stone had gone through with its assassination plot, setting off a world war.

David closed the book and took a deep breath. He knew how Hannay felt. Hannay had started out trying to prove his innocence in a murder case, but now he was racing to stop a much greater threat to his country. TopDog's computer-hacking could become a national security threat! David had to make sure he was stopped. Tomorrow, at Littleton Aerospace, he would have his chance.

Wishbone crouched low over his paws as he moved through the grass outside ToonTime Graphix Saturday morning. "No sign of Lightning or his buddies yet . . ."

He gazed toward the wide, low two-door garage behind the converted barn. Just one of the two doors was open. Wishbone spotted a jeep parked inside, but there were no greyhounds in sight.

"Looks like my buddies are inside—unless Bolton has been up to no good. Commando Dog is on the way, guys!"

Wishbone's paws were moist with dew. The sun was warm on his fur as he crept toward the sliding-glass doors. Wishbone was glad to see that they were open this morning. He looked through the doorway. Then he paused when he heard Bolton's voice coming from inside, giving Corey some instructions.

Wishbone saw Bolton and Corey bent over something on one of the desks, with their backs toward the door.

"Here's Commando Dog's chance. . . ." Wishbone advanced quickly inside. He skirted behind Bolton, keeping to the edge of the work space. His eyes darted left and right. "No dogs in the work area, or lounging on the couch . . ."

Wishbone moved as lightly on his paws as he could. He headed for the counter that separated the kitchen area from the rest of the work space. He was just a few feet away when he heard Bolton say, "Did you hear something, Corey?"

"Uh-oh." Wishbone scooted the rest of the way to the kitchen area. As he ducked behind the counter, his dog tags jingled faintly.

"What was that . . . ?" Bolton spoke up again. "Is that you, Lightning? Get out of there!"

Wishbone froze when he heard the heavy sounds of Bolton's shoes moving toward the kitchen area. He backed up, looking desperately around him. "No way out . . . And Bolton is heading this way!"

Wishbone tensed as he felt his hindquarters press into a corner. In just a second, Bolton would . . .

Brring!

The sound of the telephone made Wishbone jump.

"Now what?" Bolton's muttered voice came from the other side of the kitchen counter.

Looking up, Wishbone could see the blond hair on top of Bolton's head. Wishbone didn't dare move a single canine muscle. Across the work space, he heard Corey answer the phone.

"I'll take it up in my office," Bolton said.

His head disappeared from Wishbone's sight. A

moment later, Wishbone heard Bolton's footsteps heading up to his loft office.

"Phew! That was close!" Wishbone leaned against the wall with a sigh. But the fur along his spine was still standing on end. "Still no sign of Lightning. The enemy is on the alert, so I can't search upstairs. It looks like Commando Dog will have to set up surveillance right here."

Wishbone sniffed at the two dog dishes and water bowls that sat next to the counter island. Lightning's food dish was missing again. "I hope Lightning is all right. . . ."

David looked around as he and Gilbert followed Gilbert's Uncle Max down the hall of the main research building at Littleton Aerospace. David knew that behind every door they passed, scientists were hard at work developing the most sophisticated aerodynamic aircraft and military technology in the world. He felt lucky to have access to such an incredible place.

"Thanks a lot for helping us, Dr. Pickering," David said.

"We really appreciate it, Uncle Max," Gilbert added.

As Gilbert's uncle turned around, David felt as if he were looking at an older version of Gilbert. Like his nephew, Dr. Pickering had blond hair and wore glasses. It was easy to see that they were related.

"David, I'm Max, okay? I feel like a medical doctor when my title is used," Dr. Pickering said.

David smiled. "All right, Dr. Pick— I mean, Max. You did ask to be called by your first name last time we saw each other."

"As it happens, I'm running a heat-tolerance test on a new metal we're developing for NASA," Max told them, keeping his hands in the pockets of his white lab coat. "My assistant is overseeing the test. As long as there aren't any emergencies, I can take some time to help you."

Max pushed open a door about two-thirds of the way down the hall. He stepped back to let David and Gilbert through.

"Here we are," Max said.

"Whoa!" David's mouth fell open as he followed Max and Gilbert inside.

The room was filled with computers. One entire wall was covered with a computerized map of what looked like a military base. It was complete with a complex maze of air strips, planes, and buildings. Another screen held a detailed cross-section of a super-high-tech space shuttle. The control panels on the computers held more lights, buttons, and levers than David had ever seen. The whole room seemed to vibrate with the power of the machines.

"Cool!" Gilbert said, pointing to the huge, computerized map. "What's that, Uncle Max?"

"I'm afraid I can't give you all the details," Max said. "That's part of a classified research project we're

conducting for the Department of Defense. But I can tell you about this machine here."

David turned to see Gilbert's uncle standing next to a high-tech computer station near the door. The main console was about twice the size of the PC the F.B.I. had taken from David.

"This computer is designed to handle some of the special research needs of the scientists here," Max explained. "It's capable of locating information hundreds of times faster than ordinary computers. And we have links to resources that aren't available to most people. So . . ."

Max sat down in front of the control panel and turned toward Gilbert and David with questioning eyes.

"Where would you like to begin?"

With so much important work going on, it was hard to focus on TopDog. But then David remembered something—TopDog, too, was a threat to national security.

"The only thing that I can link to TopDog," David said, thinking over Max's question, "is the car that almost hit me yesterday."

"I thought you said the license plate was covered up," Gilbert said.

"Yes, but Joe Talbot knows something about cars, and he said it was a metallic-blue Stinger," David said. "It looked pretty new. Maybe a 1996 model, or even newer."

Gilbert's uncle nodded, typing in the information. "Let's limit the search to cars registered to owners in our part of the county. With those limits, we should be able to come up with a list of owners in no time."

He hit one last button. A fraction of a second later, a list blinked onto the computer screen. Max turned to face David, waiting for a response.

"Wow! That would've taken forever on my computer," David said.

Gilbert leaned forward and scanned the list, reading the names aloud. "Aldridge, Auerbach, Averill, Baker, Bolton . . ."

David did a double take when he heard the last name. "Bolton? Wait a sec," he said. "I think I know that guy!"

"You do?" asked Gilbert.

David's eyes jumped to the person's first name. "Hal Bolton. That's definitely him! He owns ToonTime Graphix, in town. The only reason I met him is because my friends and I found a lost dog of his. Is there a way we can find out more about him?" David asked.

Max turned back to the computer. "Let's plug in his name and—"

He turned as the door to the room swung open. A young woman with short dark hair and a lab coat hurried in, carrying a clipboard.

"I found several problems in the heat-tolerance test, Max," she said. "I think you should come right away."

Max frowned as he glanced at the clipboard she held out to him. "I'm afraid I have to take care of this matter immediately," he told Gilbert and David. "And

I can't leave you two here on your own. We'll have to stop now."

"For how long?" Gilbert asked. He stared longingly at the computer as his uncle tapped a few buttons to clear the screen.

"It could take hours," Max told him. "You two are welcome to wait. But if you want to go back to Oakdale, Littleton Aerospace has a shuttle bus service. The next bus leaves in . . ."—he looked at his wristwatch—". . . seven minutes."

David made up his mind immediately. "I have to get back to Oakdale right away," he said.

"I'll stay here," Gilbert said. "Maybe Uncle Max and I can find out more about Hal Bolton later."

"Would it be all right if I use that phone?" David asked, pointing at a telephone that hung on the wall next to the door. "I want to call my friend Joe."

Max nodded. "Sure. Just dial nine first for an outside line."

"What are you going to do?" Gilbert asked, as David reached for the phone.

"I'm not sure," David admitted. He tried to keep cool, but he could feel the adrenaline pumping through him. "But I'm not going to let TopDog get away!"

# Chapter Ten

**W**ishbone kept his eyes and ears on full alert as he sat at his post in the kitchen at ToonTime Graphix. His stomach told him it was close to lunchtime.

The terrier peeked around the side of the kitchen counter. Corey was bending over one of the computers. Bolton sat on the couch. He had a pile of paper on the coffee table in front of him.

Wishbone's ears shot up when he heard the light click-click of another canine's nails on the metal staircase. Wishbone recognized Lightning's footsteps. His surveillance had paid off! His friend was safe.

"Get away from there, Lightning!" Bolton's voice rang out through the work space. Lightning was so startled that he backed right into the coffee table. Wishbone heard a small crash. Then Bolton cried out, "Watch out!"

The fur on the back of Wishbone's neck stood up. "You'd better watch out, buddy."

A coffee cup lay on its side. Bolton slid the sheets of paper out from underneath the cup with a jerk of his arm.

Lightning let out a high-pitched whine. "Clumsy mutt!" said Bolton, shaking spilled coffee off the sheets.

"Hey! No need to get nasty with one of my canine pals!" Wishbone said, as he watched. Lightning backed away from Bolton, his four legs shaking. "You're not so graceful yourself!"

"I've had it with you! You are so clumsy—always breaking things. Why can't you behave like the other two greyhounds?" Bolton shouted, throwing the sheets of paper on the floor. "Get . . . out!"

Wishbone stiffened when he saw Bolton push Lightning toward the doors. Bolton got the greyhound outside. The terrier followed the man's every move with his ever-watchful gaze. Wishbone crouched low over his paws, ready to leap to his new friend's aid if necessary.

Bolton pushed Lightning out onto the grass. Then he slammed shut the sliding-glass doors. "Get lost! Don't come back this time!" he yelled, as he stomped past Corey and went back up the iron staircase. He hit each step with such a loud *clang* that the staircase shook.

"Commando Dog is back in action. . . ." Moving stealthily, Wishbone circled behind Corey and padded upstairs to the loft area.

"Hello?" Bolton's voice came from the office. "Is this the Oakdale Animal Shelter?"

"Animal Shelter!" Wishbone moved to the office doorway as fast as his four legs could carry him. "What's going on, Hal?"

"Officer Garcia? I have a dog that needs to be taken care of," Bolton said.

Wishbone looked up angrily at Bolton. The big wooden desk blocked most of the dog's view of the man. Suddenly, Wishbone heard a familiar voice in the work area below.

"Mr. Bolton? Are you here?"

Wishbone cocked his head to one side. "Joe!"

A moment later, he heard Joe climbing the stairs. Looking up, Wishbone spotted the phone console that he had accidentally stepped on the day before. It was right in front of his muzzle, and Bolton was facing away from it. . . .

The terrier rose up on his hind legs. He found the white button with his front paw and pressed down.

"I'm sorry to have to say this, but I can't take care of him anymore," Bolton said into the receiver.

As Bolton talked, his voice echoed clearly from the speaker on the console. ToonTime's owner was concentrating so hard on what he was saying that he didn't seem to notice.

"I had to drive all the way out to the new highway to track him down the other day. . . ."

Wishbone heard Joe's footsteps right near the office. Then the boy appeared at the doorway.

"You never tracked down Lightning, Mr. Bolton,"

111

Joe said flatly. "My friends and I were the ones who found him."

"You tell him, Joe!" Wishbone gazed across the office at Joe. He continued to hold his paw on the white button.

Bolton lowered the phone's handset and covered it with his hand. "Do you mind waiting a minute, Joe?" he said. "I'm on a private call."

"It's not private anymore," Wishbone said, glancing down at the speaker button.

Suddenly, a woman's voice echoed from the speaker on the phone console. "If you're taking proper care of your dog, he shouldn't be wandering around the highway," said Officer Garcia.

"Two times already this week," Joe said, frowning.

Bolton jerked his head around, a look of surprise on his face. "Huh . . . ? How did the speaker phone get turned on?" Bolton asked angrily. Then his gaze turned to Wishbone. "You!"

Bolton started to make a move toward Wishbone. Wishbone barked sharply at the man.

Officer Garcia's voice spoke clearly over the speaker phone again. "I'm sending a control officer over to investigate, Mr. Bolton," she said.

After letting his front paws drop to the floor, Wishbone trotted over to Joe. "Mission accomplished!" The terrier angled his head around to look up at his buddy. "So . . . what brings you here, Joe?"

David closed his copy of *The Thirty-Nine Steps* and put it in his backpack. He gazed out the window of the shuttle bus. Hannay had figured out that the thirty-nine steps mentioned in Franklin Scudder's spy notebook referred to a flight of stairs that led from a beach house at the edge of a cliff down to the sea. That was the spot where the Black Stone would make its escape by boat.

Instead of finding a gang of spies in the house, however, Hannay met a group of ordinary British gentlemen. Hannay thought he had made a mistake until he remembered "the big secret of all the famous criminals"—they didn't *look* different; they *were* different. Their appearance had nothing to do with their criminal behavior.

David was on the edge of his seat as Hannay faced the men down, looking for the cruel spies behind the pleasant masks. Slowly, Hannay recognized them as the men who had followed him across the countryside and tried to trap him in the farm house. These were the men who had killed Franklin Scudder.

As the bus approached the business district of Oakdale, David couldn't help but think about the book. He would be on the lookout for people who were not what they seemed to be.

David jumped up from his seat as the shuttle bus stopped in front of the post office. He got off the bus and jogged down the street in the direction of ToonTime Graphix. He had called Joe from Littleton Aerospace and asked him to meet him at ToonTime. He was just coming into the driveway when a horn beeped right behind him. David turned, then stepped away from the driveway to make room for a van that was pulling up in back of him.

"'Oakdale Animal Control'?" he said to himself, reading the sign on the side of the truck. "What are they doing here?"

The truck drove past David, then stopped in front of the garage behind ToonTime Graphix. Two uniformed animal-control officers got out and went to the sliding-glass doors that led into the office. As David started to follow them, his eyes fell on the garage. He thought about the sports car that had tried to run him down.

Both of the doors were closed. David walked over and tried to open them, but they were locked.

Just as David reached the sliding-glass doors, one of the animal-control officers opened them from the inside. She had dark hair that curled beneath the cap of her uniform. She led Lightning out on a leash.

David saw Hal Bolton step outside right behind her. He was talking to the other officer, a man with a muscular build.

Bolton was saying, "Summonses? Fines? That's what I get for taking in my sister's dogs when they needed a home?"

"They deserve a home with someone who *cares* about them. Based on the information Joe Talbot has given us, you have been negligent," the male officer told him.

As Bolton walked along with the two officers, he noticed David for the first time and frowned at the boy. Then he noticed Corey step through the doorway behind him. "Where do you think you're going, Corey? . . . Corey? . . . Corey!"

Corey stopped to say, "I'm just going to get some lunch, Mr. Bolton. I'll be right back." After shooting a sharp glance at David, he headed straight for the garage.

*What's going on?* David wondered. Then he spotted Joe and Wishbone standing just inside the doorway. He walked through the doorway and joined them.

"The animal shelter has received several calls about Lightning. It looks like Mr. Bolton has been trying to get rid of Lightning by abandoning him," Joe told his friend. "Thanks to those calls and Wishbone, now the Oakdale Animal Shelter is taking in all three dogs." Joe glanced at Wishbone, who stood next to the door, watching what was going on outside.

"I thought Mr. Bolton really cared about Lightning," David said. "But it was just an act."

David noticed Corey was almost at the garage.

David turned back to Joe. "Anyway, it might take more than animal-control officers to deal with Mr. Bolton." He walked over to the computer Corey had been working on.

"What do you mean?" Joe asked, coming up next to David.

"With Gilbert's uncle's help we discovered there's a metallic-blue Stinger registered to Hal Bolton—the same kind of car that tried to run me over." David shook the mouse. The image of Corey's odd cartoon spaceship came up on the screen. A cartoon ranger was just getting into it. "There might be something in here to link Mr. Bolton to the cyber-hacking."

David started to exit the animation program when the space ranger opened his mouth and cartoon words came out of it: BLASTING OFF 4 ZONDOR.

David's mouth dropped open. "Joe, look!" he said, pointing at the caption. "'Blasting off for Zondor!' That's TopDog's sign-off." David frowned as he stared at the screen. "But this is Corey's program, not Mr. Bolton's."

"So how can we tell whether TopDog is Corey or Mr. Bolton?" Joe asked.

Before David could answer, Wishbone barked loudly from the driveway. "Looks like our time's up," David said, as he looked toward the sliding-glass doors. "The animal-control truck is leaving."

"Uh-oh. Where's Mr. Bolton?" Even as he asked the question, David saw a large shadow on the grass right outside the sliding-glass doors.

"He's on his way in here!" Joe warned, as the shadow moved closer to the open doorway.

# Chapter Eleven

Just when David was sure Mr. Bolton would spot them, the man stopped in mid-stride. Wishbone was still barking in the driveway. Mr. Bolton turned away from the doorway and took a few steps in Wishbone's direction.

"We'd better get out of here," Joe said.

The boys hurried out of the building and walked toward Mr. Bolton. He turned and saw them. "Take your dog home," he said angrily. Then he began to walk back toward the converted barn. "You've caused enough trouble."

With Wishbone walking safely between them, Joe and David didn't speak until they reached the street.

"Good work, boy. Thanks for distracting Mr. Bolton." Joe reached down to pet Wishbone. "That was great timing."

Wishbone wagged his tail happily as he trotted ahead on the street. He gave a bark that seemed to say "Glad to be of service!"

118

David's mind was racing. Suddenly, he stopped and snapped his fingers. "Gilbert!" he said. "He's still out at Littleton Aerospace, trying to find out what else he can learn about TopDog. Maybe he and his uncle can help us," David said. He spotted a car turning into the parking lot of the Royal Theater, across the street. "Let's call from the theater."

A few minutes later, Joe and Wishbone stood next to David at the pay phone in the theater lobby. It seemed to take the receptionist at Littleton Aerospace forever to transfer David's call. But at last someone picked up.

"Hello. This is Dr. Pickering's office," said a voice that David recognized right away.

"Gilbert! I'm glad I got hold of you," David said.

"I just tried to call you," Gilbert answered. "I wanted to tell you what Uncle Max and I just found out." The urgency in his voice made David snap to attention.

"What?"

"Remember that metallic-blue Stinger?" Gilbert said. "Hal Bolton sold it—two days ago."

"And yesterday someone used it to try to run me down," David said.

Gilbert went on. "He sold the car to someone named—"

"Corey Anderson?" David guessed.

"How did you know?" Gilbert asked.

"Joe and I were just looking at Corey Anderson's computer. He uses the phrase 'Blasting off for Zondor.' Thanks, Gilbert," David said, as he hung up the phone.

David and Joe exchanged glances. "The car belongs to Corey. I think it's time for us to call the F.B.I."

Wishbone jumped out of the Barneses' minivan a half-hour later, into the parking lot of the Oakdale Inn. "Make way, everyone! Commando Dog and his pals are on a serious, patriotic mission!"

David, Joe, and Sam were right behind him. "Thanks for letting Joe and me come with you to talk to the F.B.I.," Sam said to David's parents, who were getting out of the front of the van.

Ruth Barnes smiled and said, "I think it's important for you to be here, too. We want to make sure we tell the F.B.I. agents every detail."

"Besides, I can use the support," David added.

Wishbone sniffed at David's hand. "We'll make sure they listen carefully."

"I still can't believe Corey was the hacker," Joe said. "And we told him you were in Wilson High's Computer Club and that you didn't have your computer anymore. That's how he found out Big Brother was David Barnes."

Wishbone trotted a short distance ahead. "How about a little credit for the dogs, folks? After all, Lightning is the one who led us to ToonTime Graphix. . . ."

"'Blasting Off for Zondor' led me to TopDog just the way the thirty-nine steps led Richard Hannay to the Black Stone," David said. He explained what the "thirty-nine steps" mentioned in Scudder's notebook meant, and how the clue led Hannay to the place where the Black Stone would meet to make its escape.

Wishbone perked up, lifting his ears to catch every word. Just thinking about Richard Hannay's adventure made the fur along his spine stand up.

David's father, Nathan, turned to his son with a serious nod. "I guess that's what we're doing, too," he said. "Stopping Corey before he makes his getaway."

Wishbone barked as they approached the big, old inn. He had been there only a few times before. As soon as they walked into the lobby, he sniffed the carpet and furniture. David's father didn't seem nearly as interested in all the interesting scents. Mr. Barnes gave his name to a man who stood behind a dark wooden counter that smelled of furniture polish.

"Agents Kendall and Guardi are expecting you," the man told Mr. Barnes. "They're in the café, down that hall."

Glancing up, Wishbone saw the man shoot a doubtful glance at him. Kicking up his paws, the dog trotted after his friends. "Hey! Wait for the dog, folks!"

Wishbone followed the scents of coffee, bread, and cold cuts down a corridor to the left of the reception desk. He caught up to his friends just as they were stepping through a doorway halfway down the hall.

"There they are," David said, nodding toward the back of the café.

Wishbone immediately spotted the two F.B.I.

agents. They sat at a round table at the back of the café, at a good distance from any other people. Two cups of coffee sat on the table in front of them. Both agents were wearing business suits.

David walked over to the table with his parents, Sam, Joe, and Wishbone.

"Hello, Mrs. Barnes, David," Agent Guardi said, standing up to shake hands.

After David introduced his father, Joe, and Sam, Agent Kendall gestured for them to sit at the table's empty chairs.

"I think my son has information that will lead you to the real computer hacker," David's father said.

"We're glad to hear that," Agent Kendall told him.

David took a deep breath. "Someone set me up," he began. "Someone my Computer Club has been talking to on-line . . ."

Wishbone gazed up at the two F.B.I. agents. They listened without saying anything, while David told them about the challenges that TopDog had given to the club members. But Wishbone noticed the sharp glances that shot back and forth between the agents when David described the on-line conversation with Blondie. Finally, David explained how TopDog might have hacked into the bank's computer system.

"Why didn't you tell us about TopDog before?" Agent Kendall asked.

David looked across the table at Agent Kendall. "I didn't think it was right to accuse someone without solid proof," he said. "I had to find out for myself

whether TopDog was the hacker before I blamed it on him."

"David didn't want to do to TopDog what someone else had done to him," Ruth Barnes added.

Agent Guardi leaned forward to take a sip of coffee. "You said you know who TopDog is?" he asked David.

"Yesterday someone almost ran me over. My friends and I traced that car and TopDog's computer signature phrase to the same person," David answered. "Corey Anderson."

"He works here in Oakdale at ToonTime Graphix," Joe added.

"Where my friend Lightning and his pals used to live." Wishbone pawed at Agent Guardi's chair.

Agent Kendall lifted a briefcase that sat on the floor

next to her chair. She opened it, pulled out a cellular phone, then got to her feet. With a nod to David, his parents, Sam, and Joe, she left the café.

"Agent Kendall will check your information," Agent Guardi explained. "We have access to the resources at the main F.B.I. headquarters by way of a laptop computer and modem in a suite. We should know every bit of available information on Corey Anderson in a matter of minutes."

"Cool," Joe said.

David and his parents looked impressed, too.

Agent Kendall returned a short time later. "Everything you told us checks out," she said.

Wishbone noticed that she didn't look like someone who'd just solved a case.

"Is something wrong?" David's father asked.

The F.B.I. agent sat back down in her chair before answering. "I just spoke to Corey's boss at ToonTime Graphix," she said. "Corey left for lunch this afternoon, and he hasn't been back since. His landlady told me that she saw him loading a suitcase and his computer into his car."

David's mouth dropped open. "You mean . . ."

Agent Kendall gave a serious nod. "It looks like Corey knew that you were on to him, David. He's gone."

# Chapter Twelve

D avid could hardly believe his ears. "Gone?" he echoed. "There must be a way to find Corey."

"You leave that to us," Agent Guardi said. The two F.B.I. agents started to get up from the table.

"Wait!" David called. "What about DynameX?"

The two agents stopped and turned to look at him. His parents looked at him in confusion.

"By experimenting with DynameX, I discovered a loophole. It was this loophole in DynameX that started all of this," David explained.

"Do you think DynameX could help us track Corey down?" Agent Guardi asked.

David nodded.

Agent Guardi ran a hand through his slicked-back hair. "Corey took his computer with him, so he must be planning to use it," the agent said. "We might be able to lure him into sending us some kind of message."

"Maybe we can find a way to use Corey's own message to track him down," David said.

The two F.B.I. agents exchanged a long look. Then, all of a sudden, Agent Kendall gave a firm nod. "Let's go up to the suite and see what we can do. . . ."

"Wow!" said David five minutes later, as he, his parents, Sam, Joe, and Wishbone stepped through the door Agent Guardi held open for them.

The space they entered looked more like a central command office than the sitting room of a hotel suite. A laptop computer and portable modem sat on a coffee table. Wires crisscrossed to the phone jack and electrical outlets. Cellular phones, files, and manuals were scattered across the chairs and tables. A map on the wall near the door was marked with color-coded notations David couldn't even try to understand. David saw CDs for half a dozen different computer programs he knew, as well as others he'd never even heard of.

"I'll have to make sure you can't access classified F.B.I. links," Agent Guardi said, as he and Agent Kendall came into the suite behind David. The agent moved to the laptop computer and typed in some commands, then made room for David, who went right to work.

"Go to it, David," Sam said, grinning.

David was glad his parents, Sam, Joe, and Wishbone were there. Having them nearby made him feel more confident.

First David telephoned Joanna's house. Shawn and Elena were there. They agreed to send him a message right away. David grinned when he saw Joanna's "Happy Birthday" message play itself out on his screen a moment later.

"That's the message she used to meet TopDog's first challenge. She programmed it by using DynameX," David said. "Now it's going to help me to challenge him."

He leaned forward and began typing.

"Look!" David sat bolt upright as something new blinked on the screen.

Agents Kendall and Guardi were next to David in a flash. "That's an e-mail address," Agent Guardi said.

David's parents came over to stand anxiously next to the agents. "What kind of address?" his father asked.

"It's Joanna's," David said. A wide grin spread across his face. "DynameX just gave me the address of the computer the anonymous message was sent from!"

"So if Corey sends us an anonymous message in a chat room, we can get his e-mail address. Nice work, David," Agent Kendall said.

Joe let out a whoop. "You did it, David! Fantastic!"

Seeing the proud looks on his parents' faces made David feel great. He felt as if he had just climbed Mt. Everest. But he knew their detective work was far from finished.

"Now comes the hard part," Agent Guardi said, crossing his arms over his chest. "Finding Corey online and getting him to send us a message."

Sam turned to the two F.B.I. agents with confused eyes. "An e-mail address isn't the same thing as a street address," she said. "How can we use that to figure out where he is?"

"Corey's Internet service is provided by a communications company," Agent Kendall told her. "The company can tell us where he's using the computer."

Agent Guardi picked up one of the cell phones from the coffee table and started to dial. "I'll take care of that," he said. With a serious nod toward the computer, he added, "David, you need to get Corey to send you a message."

David nodded. "Look out, Corey," he challenged, as he logged on to the Internet. "This time you've met your match."

David started by logging on to his Computer Club's chat room. Next he went into the chat room of Blondie's Computer Club, and even the teen talk room where Corey had interrupted his on-line conversation with Blondie. At each site he left a message that Corey would know was for him. There was no response from TopDog.

"I guess I'll try our Computer Club chat room again," David said.

David typed in the address, then clicked on the "Talk" icon. As soon as the chat room appeared on his screen, he looked at the list of people who were logged on to the site.

"Check it out!" He pointed to the last name on the list. "'Ranger,'" he said.

His mother leaned forward to look. "Who's 'Ranger'?"

"That's another code name Corey uses. He used this one when he crashed the school computers!" David said.

"Excellent," said Agent Guardi. He gestured to the cell phone cupped in the palm of his hand. "I've got our regional office on hold. It'll immediately track any address we turn up."

David felt a new burst of energy as the others gathered around him. Reaching for the keyboard, he typed: HELLO, AGAIN, RANGER. BB HERE. LOOKING 4 ME?

He sat back and waited several seconds, but Ranger didn't answer. "Come on . . ." he said under his breath.

Then David reached out to the computer keyboard again: U CLEARED OUT BEFORE WE COULD SNAG U. CLEVER MOVE. 2 BAD U WON'T GET AWAY WITH IT.

Seeing that Ranger was still logged on to the chat room, David typed a new message: U R NOT MUCH OF A HACKER WITHOUT OUR HELP.

Then he sat back, waiting. A few seconds later, Ranger's name disappeared from the list of users.

"He's logged off," Agent Guardi said. There was no emotion in his voice.

"Wait . . . look!" Joe said, as something new appeared on the screen. He pointed a finger at the multicolored helixes that spiraled around in a rectangle. These were the graphics David used in his signature.

A split-second later, words typed themselves out

inside the helixes: U WILL NEVER CATCH ME NOW. . . . I'M BLASTING OFF 4 ZONDOR!

"That's him!" Sam exclaimed.

David's fingers flew like lightning. He moved the cursor to the message and plugged in the right code. A second later, a blinking message signaled an alarm.

"Bingo!" David's father said. He grinned at the Web address that flashed on the screen.

Agent Guardi was already repeating the e-mail address into his cell phone. When he was done, he cupped his hand over the mouthpiece and said, "It should take only a matter of seconds to trace the computer that's sending the message. . . ."

All of a sudden, Agent Guardi spoke into the receiver. "Good. We're on our way."

He snapped the phone shut and turned to Agent Kendall. "Thirty-eight West Warren Road," he said.

"I know that address," David's father said. "West Warren Road is out by the old Hobrock plant. There are some warehouses there."

"I guess Corey didn't leave town," David said.

Agent Kendall was already heading for the door. She paused with her hand on the doorknob and looked over her shoulder at David, Joe, and Sam. "We might need some help identifying Corey."

"You want us to come along?" David jumped to his feet, a fresh rush of adrenaline pumping through him. "Let's go!"

Wishbone gazed excitedly out the window of the F.B.I. agents' minivan a few minutes later. "Corey doesn't stand a chance with us on his trail."

He turned to look at Joe, Sam, and David, who were sitting next to him in the van's rear bench seat. Ruth and Nathan Barnes sat in the two middle seats.

"Turn left up there," David's father said. He leaned forward to point at a wide road that angled off the street they were on. "That's West Warren Road."

Wishbone saw Agent Guardi's warning look reflected in the rearview mirror. "When we get there, you all stay put," said the F.B.I. agent. "No matter what happens, you don't leave the van. Understand?"

"Yes, sir," David said. His parents, Sam, and Joe nodded their agreement.

Wishbone thumped his tail excitedly against the seat. As Agent Guardi steered the minivan onto the road, Wishbone noticed that the smells of earth, grass, and trees faded away. Houses and lawns gave way to larger buildings made of concrete and brick.

"Number thirty-eight. Here it is." Agent Guardi pulled the van to a stop in front of a long brick building that had three wide truck-loading areas.

Wishbone gave an excited bark as he caught sight of the sports car that was parked in front of a small doorway beyond the loading areas. Sunlight glinted off its metallic-blue paint. "Red alert, guys! Corey's car!"

"Looks like Corey's still here," said Agent Kendall, nodding at the car.

Sam leaned forward and gazed at the sign above the small doorway. "'Anderson Storage,'" she read. "Isn't 'Anderson' Corey's last name?"

"This warehouse could be owned by a relative," Agent Guardi said. Keeping his eyes on the building, he opened the driver's-side door.

As Agent Guardi stepped out, Wishbone jumped onto the man's empty seat. He rose up on his hind legs and rested his front paws on the open window. "Need some help sniffing Corey out?"

Just then, the warehouse door swung outward and a young man stepped outside.

"It's Corey!" Wishbone barked.

"That's him!" David cried, pointing.

Corey was carrying a computer in his arms. When he caught sight of the minivan, he froze.

"Stay here," Agent Guardi ordered everyone in the back of the van. He whirled around to face Corey and shouted, "Freeze!"

Agent Kendall leaped out of the passenger's side, calling, "F.B.I.! Hold it right there, Corey!"

Wishbone watched as the F.B.I. agents closed in on Corey. "You're as trapped as a cat up a tree, Corey!" he said.

In the next instant, Corey took a deep breath and tried to throw his computer at the agents.

It fell just a few feet in front of Corey with a splintering crash. Corey raced toward his car.

"He's making a run for it!" David cried.

"Not with Commando Dog around!" Wishbone leaped out the open van window and onto the street. "No one said anything about the dog staying put!"

"Wishbone!" Joe called from behind him.

Wishbone's paws clacked on the pavement. Corey was still several yards ahead of him. He jumped into his car and slammed the door.

"Oh, no, you don't. . . ." Pushing off on his hind legs, Wishbone made a flying leap toward the opened car window.

Corey turned in alarm as Wishbone flew toward him. "What!" he cried.

Wishbone's hind nails scratched against the car's shiny, metallic-blue finish. Then he was inside, jumping over the seats and barking.

Corey tried to stick the key into the ignition. Before he could, Agent Kendall yanked opened the driver's-side door and grabbed Corey's arm.

"Just in time!" Wishbone told the agent.

In a matter of moments, Agent Kendall had the young man out of the car, with his hands behind his back.

Agent Guardi was right behind her. As he slapped a pair of handcuffs around Corey's wrists, Wishbone crouched over his front paws and growled up at the culprit.

"Busted!"

Wishbone wagged his tail as he trotted across the tile floor of Pepper Pete's the next afternoon. "Pepperoni pizza and garlic twists . . ." he said, sniffing the air. "I can't think of any better way to celebrate a job well done!"

Wishbone glanced up at the two tables that had been pushed together for the occasion. David, his parents and his little sister, Joe, his mom, and the four other kids in the Wilson High School Computer Club were all there. They laughed and talked as Sam and her dad came over with four pizzas and some pitchers of soft drinks.

"Those pizzas smell delicious, Walter!" Wishbone trotted around to where Joe was sitting. Rising up on his hind legs, he pawed at Joe's leg. "How about a slice for the dog?"

"This is my treat, everyone." Walter Kepler grinned as he placed two pizzas on each table. "You all deserve it after the way you worked together to catch Corey Anderson."

"I'm just glad David's name is cleared," David's father said, as he poured soft drinks into glasses and handed them out. "And Corey is taking the blame for his own computer hacking."

"Corey didn't know what he was getting into when he tried to outsmart you, David," Gilbert added. Pushing his eyeglasses up on his nose, he reached for a slice of pizza. "By the way, David, the summer conference job is still yours if you still want it."

"Yes! Thanks, Gilbert," said David.

With a smile, Sam reached down to ruffle Wishbone's fur. "I guess we've got something else to celebrate, too," she said. "Getting Lightning and the other two greyhounds taken away from Hal Bolton."

"I'll eat to that!" Wishbone said, taking the piece of pizza that Sam offered.

"I called the Oakdale Animal Shelter this morning," Ellen said. "Officer Garcia told me she already found a family that wants to adopt all three dogs."

Wishbone felt happier than ever as he gobbled up a second bit of pizza from Joe. When he looked up again, he saw that David was looking down at his plate with thoughtful eyes.

"You know what the scariest thing about this whole computer-hacking thing is?" David said. "Corey almost got away with it. It makes me realize that kind of close call doesn't happen just in the movies and in books."

"Did you ever finish reading *The Thirty-Nine Steps?*" Sam asked David. "Did Richard Hannay prove his innocence?"

David nodded. "The Black Stone turned out to be living right out in the open. Its members looked like ordinary Englishmen whom no one would suspect of any criminal acts. But Hannay learned to see through that disguise."

Wishbone cocked his head to one side, listening. "Just like you and me, David. We weren't fooled by Hal or Corey's act. Way to go!" he said.

"So the Black Stone got caught?" Sam asked.

"All of them did," Joe answered. "But not before they started a world war."

"It's a good thing we caught Corey before anything disastrous happened," David's mother said, reaching out to pat David's arm.

"Well," Joanna said, speaking up from across the table, "I don't know about any of you. But I've learned my lesson. It's going to be a long time before I have anything to do with strangers on the Internet."

Most of the others voiced their agreement. But Wishbone noticed David wasn't among them.

"I'm going to keep surfing the Net and talking to other kids on-line," David said.

Sam shot a look of total surprise at David. "Aren't you afraid the secrecy of the Net could get you in trouble again?" she asked.

"We had a bad experience with Corey," David said. "But the Internet is still an amazing way to find out things and share information. Code names and security codes are really important. They protect people's privacy."

Elena nodded her agreement as she reached for another slice from the tray. "The problem isn't that names and other information are kept secret."

"Exactly," David agreed. "It's that people like Corey don't respect the privacy that security codes are supposed to provide."

"I see what you mean," Sam said.

David took a big gulp of his drink. "Anyway, even though Corey tried to hide behind the privacy of the Internet, he ended up behind bars," he said.

"Thanks to a great team effort!" Wishbone gazed

hungrily at the fresh slice of pepperoni pizza that Joe was just placing on his plate. "How about teaming up with me to eat that pizza, Joe?"

"I guess you're right, David," Joe said. "You shouldn't let Corey's actions stop you from enjoying the Internet or your privacy."

Wishbone agreed completely. "You should never let anyone stop you from enjoying your pizza . . ."—he gobbled up the morsel of pepperoni Joe held out, then smiled around the table—". . . or your friends."

# About Anne Capeci

A nne Capeci has always loved mysteries. She has written more than a dozen of them for children, including two previous titles in the WISHBONE Mysteries series: *The Maltese Dog* and *Key to the Golden Dog*. Anne also wrote the first book in the WISHBONE Super Mysteries series, *The Halloween Joker*. Anne was glad for the chance to feature her favorite canine detective and his human pals in a new WISHBONE Mysteries title, *Case of the Cyber-Hacker*.

Anne has been fascinated by the Internet ever since she herself went on-line a few years ago. She felt the vast World Wide Web would make the perfect setting for a mystery featuring Oakdale's own computer whiz, David Barnes.

Anne got the idea for *Case of the Cyber-Hacker* after reading John Buchan's classic thriller, *The Thirty-Nine Steps*. The main character in the story, Richard Hannay, was thrown into the midst of a mystery after he had a chance meeting with a stranger. Hannay learned of an evil murder plot that could set off a world war. When he agreed to help foil the plan, the people behind the plot set him up to take the blame for a crime he did not commit. Hannay was forced to flee from the police and the plotters, his life in grave danger.

Anne decided to place David in a similar situation, after he "meets" a stranger on the Internet. The stranger turns out to be a computer hacker who sets

David up to take the blame for a cyber-crime. David is pursued through cyberspace rather than across the British countryside. Yet, just like Richard Hannay, David, Joe, Sam, and Wishbone face a dangerous threat to national security with great courage, never thinking of backing down.

Anne is not nearly as much of a computer whiz as David or the computer hacker she created in *Case of the Cyber-Hacker.* She was lucky to have the advice of several computer experts who helped her work out the details of the computer hacker's crime and David's investigation.

Anne lives and works in Brooklyn, New York, with her husband, their two children, their cat, and their computer.

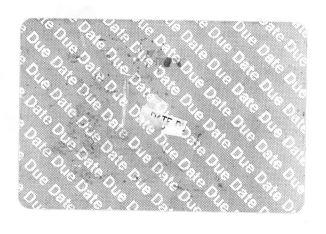